Masquerade with THE MASTER

A Master Me Novella

By Lili Valente

Masquerade with THE MASTER

By Lili Valente

———————————————

Self Taught Ninja Press

About the Book

A white hot Standalone romance from *USA Today* Bestseller Lili Valente

"Leave the mask on, princess, but everything else comes off. I'm ready to see what's mine."

They say you don't know what you've got until it's gone, but I knew long before the day I said goodbye to Ivy Prescott that I was never going to find another woman like her.

Now, we're both six years older, and my sweet, innocent Ivy has become a sexy, irresistible woman.

She wasn't ready for me then, but she's ready for me now. Ready to learn all the wicked, wonderful things I have to teach her.

Her lesson will begin with a box. A box with a beautiful dress, a mask, and an invitation to come play with a man who has been watching her from afar…

A man who wants to master her—body and soul…

Warning: This sinfully sexy read features voyeurism, bondage, and a Dominant alpha male who likes to play rough with his toys—but don't worry, he'll make sure you enjoy every scorchingly hot minute of it.

CHAPTER
One

Dear Ivy,

Are you sitting down? If you're not, I advise that you do so.

Put your feet up and get comfortable, doll. This isn't the kind of letter you want to read standing up. Yes, I'm serious. Find a seat for that fine ass of yours and take it.

Now.

There. That wasn't so bad, was it?

Maybe you even liked it. At least a little. Maybe you're intrigued. Eager to learn who has the balls to write a savvy corporate woman like you a letter like this.

I have the balls because I know you, princess. You like a man who isn't afraid to take control. You always have, even back when you were so naïve that I'm pretty sure you had no idea what I meant when I said I needed to win a woman's submission.

But you got on your knees anyway and asked me to take you to the ball.

Do you remember?

I do. I think about that night—and what a shit job I did of breaking things off—more often than I would like to admit.

But saying good-bye was for the best. I wouldn't have been good for you in the long run. Not back then. I wouldn't have been able to stop myself from taking advantage of your inexperience, no matter how hard I would have tried. We were spark and tinder, Prescott, and I would have burned you to the ground.

But things are different now...

Aren't they?

I know how you spend your Saturdays, Ivy. I know about the secret staircase, the red door, and the toys you play with in the back room with a man who wants you to call him Master. But you weren't meant for him.

You were meant for me.

If you're shaking your head—or having a hard time coming to grips with this blast from the past—ask yourself this: Whose face do you see when you close your eyes and slip your fingers between your legs? Whose hands are brushing across your nipples, smoothing over your ass, spreading your thighs wide? Whose voice is in your ear, telling you how sweet you taste, how perfectly wet you are, how much he wants to fuck you and keep fucking you until there is no doubt in your mind who your pleasure belongs to?

Tell the truth, princess. Don't lie to me, or to yourself.

Maybe you're even turned on right now. Wet. Thinking about how good we were together and all the fun we could have now that your kink has caught up with mine.

I hope so. Because I want to be with you, Ivy—in person, unfiltered, no holds barred and no holding back. I want to push your skirt up around your hips and get my mouth between your legs. I want to tie your wrists to my headboard and tease you until you beg me to take you. I want to make love to you in every filthy way you've daydreamed about and a few new ways I'll teach you because I'm a dirty bastard with a filthy mind and you are the star of every single one of my fantasies.

I want to pleasure you, possess you. I want it so bad I can almost taste the salt and honey of your skin.

No one tastes like you. So sinfully sweet...

I've been thinking so often lately about that camping trip on the beach, of that first kiss mixed with rain and the way you came on my mouth with the wind howling outside our tent. You were lightning in a bottle, and I knew that first night that I was never going to find another woman like you.

Which brings us to this moment.

This gift, and a chance to see if lightning can strike twice.

In the letter I sent with that first tuition check, I warned that there would come a day when your "anonymous friend" would ask for a favor. I also said that you would be free to say yes or no to that request—no hard feelings; no harm, no foul. I meant it then, and I mean it now. There is no debt to be repaid, only an opportunity sincerely offered.

I want to show you all the things I've learned since the night we parted ways. I want to show you how sorry I am, and how truly incredible submission can feel. That man you've dabbled with doesn't have what it takes to top you, but I do. Meet me tonight and let me prove it.

You're ready for the ball, princess, and I would so very much like to be the man to take you.

I'll send a car at eight.

Sincerely,
Edward

CHAPTER
Two

Ivy

Good God...*Edward.*

I stand up only to sit down hard again, my tailbone twinging as it meets the wooden seat of the chair.

Edward is my mysterious benefactor, the man who paid for my last year of undergraduate school and the master's program after. The one who set me up with ten thousand dollars in startup money to fund my move to New York City and keep me in coffee and ramen noodles while I interned, before I landed an entry-level advertising job. He's the one who sent chocolates and champagne when I was promoted the first time, and Broadway tickets when I made Assistant Creative Director last month.

The tickets had come in an antique jewelry box, along with a note saying "I never doubted you for a moment. Congratulations on your success. –Anon."

Anon, short for Anonymous, but I'd thought I'd known who was looking out for me. My brother Aaron might be a selfish shit most of the time, but he loves me. He would never stand by and let our parents steal my inheritance and disown me without taking steps to make things right.

Or so I'd thought.

But if Edward is the one behind the money and the gifts…

If Edward is behind all of this, then that means…

I drop my face into my hands, letting my fingers muffle a long, low groan. "Jesus, Aaron. You sorry son of a bitch."

My older brother isn't a jerk with a secret heart of gold after all. He's just a jerk—a selfish, self-serving bastard who was happy to turn his back on me because it was easier than standing up for what was right. I've spent years writing him thoughtful emails and tolerating his half-hearted replies for nothing. Aaron was never my ally or my friend. He's just another person I'm unlucky enough to call family.

I swallow hard, ignoring the pressure building behind the bridge of my nose.

I won't cry. Not for him or any other Prescott. I made a promise to myself years ago, after my gram died, not to give my shitty family any more of my tears. This fresh sucker punch hurts, but the pain will fade. It's the idea of a benevolent big brother that I'll miss. In reality I'm not any more alone than I have been for the past six years.

Aaron hasn't been there for me in a long time, not since Mom and Dad tore up Gram's will, bribed her crooked attorney, and kicked me out of the house for trying to "take what belonged to them." I hadn't even known Gram was naming me sole heir, but that hadn't mattered to my parents. The money was all they cared about. And apparently the same goes for Aaron.

I'm not losing a brother; I'm gaining an extra hour every other weekend. No more afternoons writing emails means more time to enjoy myself.

To *enjoy* myself...

My gaze shifts from the letter to the cream box on the kitchen table. It's two feet wide and three feet long, tied up with a red satin bow. It's also heavy and I'm guessing expensive, judging by the Bergdorf-Goodman logo on the bag it arrived in. It was delivered twenty minutes ago by courier, along with a hand-written letter.

A letter from *Edward Mulligan*, the boy I crushed on for most of my teenage existence, the man who took my virginity in a tent by the sea, the asshole who was so wonderful and romantic that I fell madly in love with him, only to have him tell me my love wasn't enough.

I wasn't enough.

And you weren't. You weren't ready for a man like Edward. Can you imagine if you'd received a letter like this back when you two were dating?

You would have fainted.

Or burst into tears.

Or run, the way you ran that night…

I pick up the letter, scanning it again with narrowed eyes. Dirty-talking, game-playing, dress-ripping Edward is back.

Even a couple of years ago, I would have said I hated him.

But now…

Now I'm a full-fledged, fucking grown-up. I've held down a challenging job, landed two promotions, negotiated a raise with my intimidating boss, Mr. Tennyson, and perfected a "you don't want to mess with me, buddy" glare that keeps all but the most determined New York City creepers at arm's length. I've also learned to ask for what I want in the bedroom, and that I enjoy regular walks on the wild side.

I'm a regular at a members-only club for Dominants and submissives, and I know how much wicked fun there is to be had in the dark. After the past few years of experimentation, there's no way I could go back to making sweet, innocent love to an earnest virgin.

It no longer surprises me that Edward called things off. I'm more surprised that he started a relationship with me in the first place. I was so innocent, so naïve, and so pathetically in love with my older brother's best friend, the only man in my life who didn't treat me like I was made of glass.

My grandfather was the first famous televangelist of the 1980s. My father followed in his footsteps, and my mother made it her job to be the perfect preacher's wife, which meant molding me into the perfectly pure, squeaky-clean preacher's daughter. Edward was right in his letter. I was so sheltered I didn't understand what BDSM was until months after our breakup. It took much longer for me to work up the courage to explore my fantasies, to find out if my daydreams about being taken by a Dominant man were something I would enjoy in real life.

Master Hansen, the man who has topped me for the past six months, teases that I'm a cliché—the fallen preacher's daughter, the good girl determined to go bad. But it goes deeper than that. Growing up, I had no choice but to submit to the powerful men in my life. Now, submission makes *me* feel powerful.

I make the choices. I choose when, where, how, and to whom I offer my obedience and the privilege of giving me pleasure and pain.

If I go to Edward, it will be *my* choice, nothing forced upon me by anyone else.

My skin goes electric at the thought. If I take him up on his offer, in less than six hours I could be kneeling at Edward's feet, kissing Edward's lips, coming on Edward's incomparable cock.

Back when I was a twenty-year-old virgin, I had no idea that all cocks are *not* created equal. If I'd known then that I would never find another man capable of making me come like a steam engine careening off the tracks, maybe I would have fought through my shame and stayed with him that night.

The thought makes me snort aloud.

I flick the letter into the air, sending it

sailing up to hit the light fixture before it lands with sharp tick on the glass table. My cat, Shiver, who is not accustomed to me throwing things, exits the kitchen, stage right, with a hiss of disapproval.

"Sorry," I call after her, but my heart isn't in it.

In my mind I'm not in my Brooklyn apartment with my cat. I'm back at the gates of the Castle of Sin on the night of the Venus Ball. I'm back at Edward's side when he ripped the front of my dress open and told me to play with my nipples while the rest of the people waiting to get into the ball watched.

It was the first time I'd ever been naked in public in my entire life. Even if I had forced myself to obey and survived the embarrassment of touching myself in front of those masked people, what Edward wanted to do to me inside the walls of that "castle" would have scared me out of my mind.

He was right. Twenty-year-old Ivy wasn't ready to play with the big boys.

But twenty-six-year-old Ivy...

Before I can second-guess my decision, I tug the red ribbon free and open the box. Inside, cradled in a nest of tissue paper, is a black masquerade mask and the most beautiful dress I've ever seen. It's a slinky black floor-length number with tiny crystals sewn over every inch and a see-through panel that starts just below the deep V of the neck, tapers to the waist, and then veers off to expose part of the hip before trailing all the way to the floor.

The fabric hisses softly as I pull the dress from the paper and hold it up to the light. I can already tell that it will fit perfectly, and that it will bare more flesh than I've ever bared in public. The neckline plunges into a V so deep, I can't imagine how the girls are going to stay contained. I'm on the larger side of a D cup and usually require some serious elastic to keep me decent.

But then, Edward clearly doesn't want me decent. He wants me naughty and half naked and willing to let him do wicked, kinky things to me.

A mental image flashes through my mind—Edward's dark hair falling over his forehead into his even darker eyes. His smile like a slash of light in the darkness as he beckons me closer and pulls me in for a kiss, a kiss that goes on and on until I'm so breathless I don't offer any resistance when he guides me onto my knees in front of him and opens his fly, telling me it's time to show him what I've learned in all our years apart.

My tongue tingles at the thought, and a rush of saliva fills my mouth. I never had the pleasure of taking Edward's cock between my lips—I was too shy back when we were a couple—but God, I want to. I want to give him the blowjob of his life, leave him weak-kneed and so shattered by pleasure he won't know what hit him. I want to see how fast he'll recover from the things my tongue can do to him, and his reaction when he realizes that I learned to suck cock from someone other than him.

Dangerous thoughts, Ivy.

Nothing says "I'm still not over you" like trying to make a guy jealous of the other cocks you've sucked.

I press my lips together. It's true. And the last thing I want to do is give Edward any reason to think I've been pining for him. He's clearly still cocky enough without any encouragement, and I have no interest in anything more than sex. I learned my lesson the first time about giving my heart to a guy like Edward.

If I'm going to do this, I'll have to go in with ground rules. For Edward and myself.

As I shower and dry my hair, I think about what it will take to keep this night about kinky experimentation and nothing more. By the time I've put on my makeup, slipped into the dress, which makes my body look made for sin, and donned my mask, I have a game plan.

In the car on the way to the ball, as the driver speeds out of the city and into the foothills of upstate New York, I'm nervous but confident. I can handle this. I can have a night of fun with a man who knows what to do with the ten inches he's been blessed with, enjoy myself, and walk away.

I owe Edward that much for all the help he's given me, and I owe it to myself to prove that I've grown up and grown out of Mr. Mulligan.

He's right—his *is* the face in my erotic dreams. His are the hands I imagine touching me when I'm alone in my bed with nothing but the ceiling fan whirring overhead and my vibrator buzzing between my legs

But tonight, all of that is going to change. Tonight Edward can have me in every wicked way he wants, and I'll give as good as I get. I will ride him all night long, sex him out of my system, and wake up tomorrow a free woman, no longer haunted by the ghosts of Things That Were Never Meant to Be.

I feel good. Great, even.

As the car pulls down the paved driveway to where the gothic Castle of Sin looms on a hill, surrounded by the stone walls that enclose its pleasure gardens, I'm not the least bit nervous. The well-dressed people lining up for entrance don't scare me, either. I'm older, dressed as well as any of these wealthy women, and I've got two years of experience as a submissive under my belt. I'm not going to embarrass myself or run away. I'm going to prove that I belong here.

I am confidence personified...right up to the moment strong hands grab me from behind, lifting me off the path and tugging me back into the dark.

CHAPTER

Three

Edward

From my hiding place behind a stand of bayberry bushes near the castle walls, I spy Ivy the moment she gets out of the car. She's even more beautiful than I remember, her red-brown hair falling in wild curls around her shoulders, her lips stained pink, and her full hips swaying back and forth in that incredible dress.

She's a goddamned heart attack waiting to happen.

The second I lay eyes on her, I know I won't be able to wait until we're alone in the garden. I need to touch her. Now. Six years without her skin against mine is too long for me to exercise restraint.

As she passes by my hiding place, I step out, wrapping an arm around her waist, lifting her off the ground as my free hand covers her mouth.

She stiffens and sucks in a surprised breath, but relaxes when I whisper "Don't worry, it's me," and draw her deeper into the shadows behind the bushes.

The curve of her ass presses against where I'm already hard, and we both moan, the twin sounds of need making me smile into her curls.

"That answers my first question," I murmur, flattening my hand low on her stomach, blood catching fire as the sweet, familiar, too-long-without-her smell of Ivy floods my head.

"And what is that, you sneaky bastard? You almost gave me a heart attack!"

"And that answers my second," I say, trying not to be too disappointed. She has every right to be angry with me, after all. "I understand if you hate me, princess. But I hope you'll give me a chance to make amends."

"I don't hate you." Her breath hitches as my hand slides even lower, hovering above the apex of her thighs. "I don't feel anything for you anymore, Edward. I'm just here for a good time."

"Me, too," I lie as I sweep her hair from her neck and press my lips lightly to her throat. "And I'm glad you don't hate me. I enjoy not being hated."

I don't mention anything about love or regret or how much I want this to be about more than fun. I knew when I wrote that letter that tonight wasn't going to be easy.

But then, the best things never are.

She swallows, her muscles working beneath my lips. "Me, too. But before this goes any further, I need to make one thing clear: we keep this casual, okay? I'm a busy person, and I'm not interested in more than one night and an easy good-bye. If you're looking for a steady date, or hoping to rekindle old flames, I'm not your girl."

My chest tightens at her words. She's always been the girl for me. I'd just needed her to become her own girl first. She was so damned young, even for a twenty-year-old. I had to give her time. I needed her to gain experience, confidence, and the strength to tell me to go to hell when I try to take things too far.

Because I always take things too far, and I'm afraid tonight won't be an exception. I know I should keep heavy stuff off the table until I've proven to Ivy that I deserve another chance, but my heart is already pounding out that fierce, possessive rhythm it beats whenever this woman is around.

She's *mine*. She belongs here with her body warm and soft in my arms and her breath coming faster simply because we're standing this close.

"Did you hear me, Ed?"

"Watch it, Prescott," I warn, but there's a smile in my voice as I curl my fingers, pressing lightly against her clit through her sexy-as-sin dress. "You know I hate nicknames. Call me Ed again, and I'm going to spank you."

She turns, meeting my gaze over her shoulder. "Is that a promise?"

My cock swells thicker at the challenge. No doubt about it, Ivy is all grown up and hot as fucking hell.

"If you want it to be." I shift my hips forward until my erection is nestled between the cheeks of her ass.

"Oh, I do. I want the full package, Mulligan, no holding back," she says, voice breathy. "I want what you promised in your letter."

"And you're going to get it. Anything you want tonight. Anything you need. I'll redden your ass, tie you up, and show everyone how sexy you are when you come on my mouth." She shivers, giving me all the encouragement I need to add, "And then I'll take you—right there in the grass because I won't be able to wait to get back to our room."

"No sex where other people might see," she says. "That's my hard limit. I don't go that far in public."

I nudge her clit with my finger again, humming beneath my breath. "Does that include no fucking you with my tongue? I'll confess I'm attached to the idea of devouring you while you're naked in the moonlight."

"Oral is okay." Her eyelids flutter as I increase the pressure between her legs. "But nothing else. It's too…"

I draw her dress up, fisting the heavy fabric in my hands, baring her thighs by slow degrees. "Too?"

"Dangerous," she says, shivering again. "We shouldn't both be out of control. One of us needs to keep their head on straight."

"I won't be out of control." I reach her panties and run my finger over the satin, loving the heat I can feel coming off of her sex. Fuck, she's already so hot for me, and I intend to make her even hotter. "Even when I'm balls deep in you, I'm going to be in control. In control of your pleasure and your pain and this beautiful pussy." I pull the crotch of her thong to one side and slide a finger through her wetness. "Damn, sweetness. Is all of this for me?"

"No, it's for the other guy who's got his hand in my panties," she says, making me smile again. "What about you, Edward? Any hard limits?"

"Only one." I press two fingers inside her, penetrating her swollen flesh, my balls aching as she gasps and widens her stance, giving my hand room to move between her legs. I can't wait to be inside her, to be thrusting more than my fingers deep into this woman who drives me wild like no other.

But first I need her consent to play. "Once we step through the gates, I'll be in charge. I call the shots; I name the games. And from the moment we start a scene until we finish, you will call me sir or Master and make it your mission in life to please me. Do you understand?"

"I know how to play, sir," she says, giving me a taste of how incredible it will be to have her submission. "These days I understand what Dominance means, but I don't go inside without a safe word."

"Name it." I lean back against the wall, and

Ivy leans back with me, propping one foot on the stones, granting me even greater access to the paradise between her thighs, access I take advantage of as I drive in deeper, harder.

"My safe word is 'marionette.'" Her breath comes fast as she shifts her hips, meeting my thrusts. "And I'm serious. This is sex. Nothing more. We're not picking up where we left off."

"I understand." I silently amend that understanding is something fluid and subject to change.

"And that means no hurt feelings or—" Her words cut off as I thumb her clit, rubbing her until she moans. "Oh God, that feels good."

"And there's so much more," I promise. "I'm going to make you come until you think you can't take any more. Then I'm going to make you come again. And again. Until you beg me to stop. But I won't stop, because I intend to have no fucking mercy when it comes to your pleasure tonight."

She reaches back, fingers tangling in my hair. "Jesus, Edward. I'm going to come right now."

"Not yet, beautiful." I glance down to see her right breast peeking out of the plunging neckline of her dress, and I bite my lip. Her nipple is bare to the cool air, and I want to suck it into my mouth more than I've wanted anything in years.

But suffering is good for the soul, and delaying satisfaction makes the payoff that much sweeter.

"Any more conditions?" I ask.

"Conditions," she echoes, her nails digging into my scalp. "I can't remember. I can't think of anything but how much I want you. Can I come, Edward? Please? I need to so badly."

"Not yet." I find her nipple and roll the bud between my fingers, loving the soft, hungry sound she makes in response. "Wait for me. Wait until I give you permission."

She moans and arches closer to my hands. "I'm trying, but the way you touch me... God, Edward, it's like no one else. You feel so insanely good."

"You too, princess," I say, heart squeezing tight in my chest. "I can't wait to make you scream."

"Yes," she murmurs. "Oh, yes, please. Please!"

"Then come for me, baby. Come on my hand. Let me feel you get off."

Her head falls back, her pussy locking down around my fingers as she calls my name in a choked voice.

"Fuck, yes, Ivy," I murmur into her hair, my cock throbbing against her ass. "Just like that. I love watching you come. You're the sexiest thing I've ever seen."

She gasps, pulling in a deep breath as her body continues to grip my fingers. I slow my strokes, waiting until I feel her relax against me before I slide my hand from between her legs.

I hold her for a long moment, counting the beats of her heart as the pulse at her neck slows, before I lower her dress and turn her gently in my arms.

She tilts her head back, looking slightly dazed. "Well, that was a hell of a greeting."

I smile. "Sorry. I couldn't help myself. Have I told you how beautiful you look tonight?"

The heat glittering in her eyes cools. "Thank you. But you don't have to flatter me, remember."

"It's not flattery, it's the truth. You're beautiful. Completely stunning from head to toe. Even prettier than that night on the beach."

Her lips press together in a thin line. "I have one more condition. No talking about the past, or dredging up the past, or analyzing the past. Tonight, we live in the here and now."

"I like it when you're stern with me." I cup her bottom through her dress, squeezing lightly. "Like a sexy schoolmarm."

"I'm serious, Edward," she says, frown still firmly in place.

"I realize that, Prescott." I incline my head. "I accept your final condition, though I have to confess you're making me wonder what sort of submissive you are. Do the Masters at your playroom let you boss them around like this?"

"Of course not." Her lips curve. "But they're experienced, accustomed to topping a woman who knows what she wants and how she wants it."

I grin, and my cock pulses against her hip, silently assuring her that it's up for the challenge of topping her anywhere, anytime. "Are you saying you doubt I've got what it takes to earn your submission, sweetheart?"

She shrugs. "I don't know, Mulligan. For all I know you've gone soft in your old age. You're pushing forty now, right?"

"I'm thirty-two, and you know that perfectly well, brat," I say pleasantly, swatting her lightly on the bottom. "And I haven't gone soft. Quite the opposite, in fact."

"So it seems," she murmurs, rocking her

hips closer to my aching length. "Would you like me to do something about that before we go in?"

"No, thank you." I brush a curl from her cheek. "A thoughtful offer, but I'm a patient man. And I need to make you come a few more times before I fuck your pretty mouth."

Her eyes darken. "All right. You're calling the shots."

"That I am." I thread my fingers through hers. "Your safe word is marionette, your hard limit is public intercourse, and you insist I refrain from talking about the past or falling helplessly in love with you. Is that all I need to remember?"

She smiles, a wry grin that makes me think the past isn't as far from her thoughts as she would like me to believe. "That's it, sir."

"Then after you, madam." I gesture toward the path.

She brushes her hair over her shoulder and adjusts her mask, hesitating a moment before she adds in a softer voice, "Thank you, by the way. For everything you did for me."

"You are so very welcome. It was truly my pleasure." I bring a hand to her cheek, fingers brushing the satin mask, hoping there will come a time when there is no need for rules or disguises.

That there will come a day when Ivy is mine, the way she was meant to be.

CHAPTER
Four

Ivy

*R*emain calm. *You must remain calm.*

If you freak out the way you did last time, you will never forgive yourself. Just relax, get a drink in your hand, and try to forget that you're about to do things in front of hundreds of people that you've only done in the dark.

Oh, and that you'll be doing them with Edward, *who is even more insanely sexy than he used to be, and who is probably going to break your heart into a thousand tiny, jagged pieces all over again because your self-control is absolute shit when you're with this man.*

"Fuck me," I mutter, fighting to breathe past the knot of anxiety in my throat.

"What was that?" Edward tucks my hand more firmly into the curve of his arm as we move down the walkway, toward the castle on the hill.

"Fun," I say, forcing a smile. "This is going to be fun."

He chuckles, making me think he knows exactly what I said and exactly how nervous I am—he always could read me like no one else—but before I can come up with a more clever response than "shut up, asshole," we've reached the end of the line of couples waiting to enter the Venus Ball.

My tongue slips out to wet my lips as I shift to my left, peeking past the man in front of me to catch a glimpse of the castle gates and the grounds beyond. Past two enormous men in red masks checking invitations, I see what must be acres of gardens, illuminated by lanterns and torchlight. Paved pathways wind through the carefully manicured bushes, flowers, and ornamental trees. The stones shine like freshly polished shoes, and the cool air is perfumed with night flowers. I catch the scent of jasmine and something softer— tuberose or phlox—on the breeze, and the tension stitched between my ribs loosens.

A little.

If all else fails, I can distract myself with botany. Thanks to Gram—the only truly sweet soul in my family full of professed saints—I know the names of almost every common North American flower and plant. Helping her in the garden was my favorite escape as a child, and gardens have felt like safe havens ever since.

Maybe not after tonight…

I push the thought away, concentrating on drawing smooth breaths, making each exhalation longer than the inhalation. It's a technique I learned in graduate school, a way to trick the parasympathetic nervous system into chilling the hell out before I had to get up in front of a class of two hundred freshmen to teach Digital Marketing 101. I've never been a fan of public speaking. Maybe it was all those years of sitting with my ankles crossed in the front row while my father boomed about hellfire from the pulpit and cameras rolled on his loyal family that bred distaste for being the center of attention.

Or maybe it's just a coincidence. Public speaking is one of the most common phobias. Public fucking would probably be pretty high on that list, too, if more people attended functions like these.

"Almost there, Prescott," Edward whispers for my ears only. "If you're turning back, turn back now."

I lift my chin. "Not a chance. But if you're

having second thoughts, I understand."

"My only thoughts involve you, this dress on the ground, and my mouth on every inch of you," he says, sending a bolt of heat knifing through my belly.

He's already made me come harder than I have in years and we haven't made it inside the damned party yet. No matter how little I enjoy the thought of taking it all off in front of strangers—I've never removed more than my coat outside of a private room at my club—no amount of "naked in public" anxiety can make me turn back before I've gotten more of Edward. More of his hands and his mouth and that long, hard, ridiculously perfect cock.

"Shall we start with the restraint wall near the castle?" Edward asks, his hand warm at the small of my back as the line shuffles forward.

The restraint wall... Jesus, am I going to be tied up right next to one of these other women? How is that not going to be awkward as hell?

"I've never played in the public space at my club," I confess, deciding that giving him a heads-up isn't admitting weakness. Only two couples separate us from the gates, and despite the chill in the spring air my palms are starting to sweat. "I've always paid for a private room."

"I know," Edward says calmly.

I frown behind my mask. "How do you know? Just how closely have you been watching me?"

"Very closely." He pats my hip, as if confessing he's been stalking me isn't weird at all. "I wanted to make sure you were safe. I know your father has his share of enemies. I wanted to make sure you weren't caught in the crossfire."

I relax, outrage fading. "When you put it that way, it's hard to stay angry at you for being a creepy spy."

He turns to me with a smile. "Well, what if I told you that I paid your friend, Master Hansen, a visit? And that I promised to cut off his hands if he touches you again?"

My eyes go wide. "You didn't."

"No, I didn't." He laughs. "But I thought about it. He's too old for you."

"He's thirty-nine." My lips curve as I cock my head, studying his profile. "And since when are you the jealous type?"

"Since I spent six years waiting to make things right with you," he says, surprising me all over again. "Like I said in the letter, I'm sorry I was an ass the last time we were here.

And I'm sorry I severed ties so completely. At the time, it seemed like the best decision, but in hindsight I realize how hard it must have been for you to lose the last link to your past."

I stand up straighter. "It's fine. More than fine. You subsidized my entire life for years, for God's sake. If anyone owes someone an apology it's me."

"What in the world would you need to apologize for?"

I bring my fingers to the edge of my mask, grateful for the help concealing my expression. "I thought Aaron was the one sending me money. If I'd known it was you, I wouldn't have accepted so much help. At least not without a few hundred thank-yous and a promise to pay back every penny. Which I will, by the way. As soon as I can. With interest."

He makes a sound somewhere between a cough and a snort. "You will not. I don't need your money, Ivy. I already have more than I know what to do with."

"But I need to pay you back," I insist, fully aware that Edward has the kind of fortune that not even a compulsive gambler can burn through in a generation.

And Edward has never been a gambler. He's careful and thoughtful, the kind of person who thinks ten steps ahead and twenty years down the road. By twenty-three he had already doubled his family's net worth, and since then he's opened a chain of wildly successful night clubs and a few luxury hotels.

Hell, the tickets to this ball probably cost more than I make in a year, but that's not the point.

"When I thought it was coming from the money Gram intended for me, I could accept it," I continue. "I thought it was coming from family and—"

"I am family." He cuts me off, his words sending regret rushing through my chest.

There was a time when Edward *was* like family to me. He was the kinder, funnier big-brother figure I'd crushed on all through high school, spending the long weekends when he visited our house daydreaming about what it would be like to have him take me behind the pool house and kiss me until I was breathless.

And then, my junior year of college, he had. And for six beautiful months it had felt like all my silly, romantic fantasies were coming true.

But all it had taken was one long weekend to lose it all—my family, my faith, my boyfriend, and all my stupid dreams.

"No, Edward," I say, gently but firmly.

"You're not family. You're not even my friend. Not anymore. We haven't been in touch for years. You may have been having me followed, but that doesn't mean you know me. And I don't know you." I force a smile. "But that's okay. I don't have to know you to have a good time tonight."

He sighs. "Ivy, I—"

"I'm prepared to give you my submission," I continue, needing to get the words out before it's too late. "But that's the only thing on the table. Please don't forget that."

A muscle in his jaw leaps, but there's no time for him to respond.

We're at the front of the line. It's time to leave reality at the gate and step into another world.

CHAPTER
Five

Edward

The part of me that's determined to prove that the connection between us is as strong as ever wants to bypass the gardens, drag Ivy up to the elegant old building on the hill, find our room, and fuck her until she's too weak with pleasure to shut me out. She confessed that no one has ever made her feel the way I make her feel. My gut tells me all it would take is an hour or two alone in the dark to tear down the wall she's built between us.

And there are so many ways I want to have her.

I want Ivy on top of me, grinding on my cock as I suck and bite and tease her nipples with my tongue. I want her from behind with my hand in her hair and my balls slapping against her thighs. I want her up against a wall, her breath coming sharp and fast because I'm fucking her so hard she can barely breathe, so hard that when she comes her orgasm will whip through her like a tornado, shattering her defenses.

And then I want to make love to her slowly, to take my time worshipping her body, showing her how grateful I am for every beat of her heart.

But if we go that route, we might never make it out to play, and the Venus Ball comes but once a year. I can't pass up the chance to top Ivy, and—glutton for punishment that I am—I like that she's not going to make it easy for me.

I was born with a silver spoon in my mouth and the world at my feet. I could have sat back, propped up my shoes, and let the abundance flow in without the slightest bit of effort. Instead, I work five days a week and the occasional weekend, slowly building my family's fortune into an empire. I prefer to earn my rewards the old-fashioned way, with balls-to-the-wall hard work.

So instead of starting up the hill, I guide Ivy down the garden path toward the lily pond and the Japanese bridge leading to the sculpture garden. Since the day I decided to send this invitation, I've been daydreaming about Ivy intertwined with one of my favorite statues, and I'm past ready to make fantasy a reality.

"What do you know about Athena?" I ask, setting a slow, deliberate pace. The night is still young, and the games usually start slow. But two hours from now, the entire garden will echo with the sounds of people letting go of their inhibitions.

"I know she was born from Zeus's forehead after he swallowed her mother." Ivy lifts her skirt, climbing the steps of the sharply arched bridge. "She was the goddess of wisdom and war, an expert strategist, and had a bad habit of helping shore up the patriarchy, siding with the boys' club even when her father was being a huge fucking dick."

I laugh, not surprised that Ivy knows her Greek goddesses. She was raised in an evangelical household, but the girl read everything she could get her hands on. At sixteen, she'd been one of the most well-read people I'd ever met. By the time she was twenty, she was a fascinating mix of innocence and self-taught genius, a clever girl with a sharp mind and the beginnings of the foul mouth she's clearly continued to cultivate since then.

"Zeus *was* a huge fucking dick," I agree. I stop at the top of the bridge, gazing out across the grounds and the moon rising above the trees. "I never liked him."

"Me, either. He was way too rapey," Ivy agrees, making me laugh. "What? He was."

"I know, I just…" I let my words drift off as I turn back to her. She's stunning in the moonlight, her pale skin as flawless as any of the statues in the sculpture garden.

"But that wasn't your point, was it?" She adjusts the lapel of my tux, smoothing it flat. It's an affectionate touch, one that gives me hope this won't be my only night with the stunning woman she's become.

"Not really, but it's relevant." I take her hand. "I was thinking about the story of Athena and Medusa. Do you know it?"

She shakes her head. "I didn't realize they had a story. This is the same Medusa who had the hair made of snakes, right?"

"The same." I twine my fingers through hers. "But that wasn't always true. Before she was a monster, Medusa was a priestess in service to Athena. A beautiful girl, so heartbreakingly lovely that she spent most of her time hiding out in the shrine, doing her best to avoid various rapey individuals."

Ivy shakes her head. "Those Greek ladies couldn't catch a break, could they?"

"Sadly, no. But Medusa did her best. She was very devout and determined to remain a virgin, one of the prerequisites for serving Athena."

Ivy huffs. "I would have chosen Aphrodite. Or Bacchus, the god of wine." She glances past me at the garden, where the only movement comes from a breeze blowing through the limbs of a willow tree.

One of the best parts of the Venus Ball is the sheer size of the venue. The Castle of Sin—formerly the Abbey of Mount Pleasant, a monastery that became a secret erotic retreat for the wealthy in the early seventies—is surrounded by sixty acres of gardens, and I know all the best places to hide. If we're lucky, Ivy and I won't set eyes on anyone but each other until we make our way to the main building later tonight.

"There is wine at this shindig, isn't there?" Ivy asks. "I hope this isn't one of those parties where they make you smuggle in your own flask, because I left my hollowed-out-Bible with the whiskey hidden inside at home."

"Your father would be scandalized."

"Why do you think I picked a Bible instead of *The Complete Works of Shakespeare*?"

I return her wicked grin. "There's an open bar inside the castle and another in the courtyard outside. But we won't be drinking until later. I want your submission straight up, princess, without anything to cloud your mind except how much you want me."

She studies me from the corner of her eye. "I get that. But I can handle my liquor now, Edward. I'm not a kid who gets dizzy from a glass of champagne. I can down two happy-hour margaritas and a beer at the pub and still stay awake for the entire cab ride home."

"Very badass."

She wrinkles her nose, sending her mask rising higher on her face. "I am very badass. And I'm going to prove it to you. But first I want to hear the rest of the story. What happened to Medusa? How did she go from beautiful young priestess to hideous monster?"

I nod. "Right. So one day Poseidon, the god of the ocean, was swimming by the shrine and got an eyeful of Medusa while she was gathering flowers outside. Instantly, he knew he had to have her. He tried to seduce her away from the holy life, begging her to abandon her vows and become his lover, but she refused. Finally, he got tired of asking and decided to take what he wanted. He hid in the shrine, waiting until Medusa was alone at the altar, then he emerged from the shadows and raped her on sacred ground."

Ivy's jaw drops. "Bastard!"

"And it gets worse, unfortunately," I confess. "Instead of taking vengeance on behalf of her priestess, Athena blamed Medusa for defiling her temple, insisting the girl should have done a better job of hiding her beauty. She flew into a rage and cast a spell, transforming Medusa into a monster so hideous that one glance at her turned men to stone."

Ivy's breath rushes out and genuine sadness flickers in her eyes. "What utter bullshit. Why don't women stand up for each other, Edward? Why do they keep making excuses for men and blaming the victim?"

"It's just a story, Prescott," I say gently, even as I curse myself for forgetting that there is a more tender than average heart beneath Ivy's tough-girl act.

"It's not just a story. It's terrible, and women defending women hasn't come nearly far enough in the past twenty-five centuries. Sisters need to stick up for each other."

"Or we could, as a society, take steps to discourage assault. Better to prevent the crime in the first place, don't you think?"

"Well, of course," she says, rolling her eyes as we start back across the bridge, "but like *that's* going to happen anytime soon. Have you been following the news lately? Rapists get off with a slap on the wrist all the time, but most people couldn't care less."

I frown. "I care."

She waves a dismissive hand. "But you're not normal, Edward. You never have been."

It's clear she means the words as a compliment, but they still send anger flashing through my chest. "Well, I should be. And as soon as I get home, I'm writing a check to a charity that fights violence against women. A big check."

"That's nice of you, but..." She sighs, pulling away from me at the base of the bridge. "But I'm afraid I'm missing your point. Why tell such a sad story, Mulligan? Are you trying to kill the mood?"

I recapture her hand, giving it an apologetic squeeze. "Not even a little bit. Killing the mood is the last thing I want to do." I tug her around the next curve in the path, into a tunnel of arched tree limbs lit by flickering torches. "I told you because I wanted you to know why the place I'm taking you is so special to me."

Halfway down the path, I make a sharp

turn between two urns into an even darker tunnel formed by carefully manicured holly bushes. This path is nearly pitch black, lit by nothing but the moonlight visible at the other end of the shadowed passage.

Ivy hesitates, gripping my hand tighter. "What place?"

"Come with me. See for yourself." I step into the darkness and she follows, putting her trust in me the way I hoped she would.

But I have to be more careful from here on out. I don't want to do anything to put a damper on her first time at the ball. I want her to remember tonight as one of the sexiest, most fulfilling nights of her life. I want her to be eager to return with me next year, and the year after, until we've explored every secret corner of the estate and I've shown her just how enchanting this place can be.

A few moments later, we step out of the dark, emerging into the sculpture garden, where pale marble statues stand watch over the courtyard like guardians made of moonlight and bone.

Ivy's breath catches. "Oh, Edward, it's…" She shakes her head, sending her curls drifting around her shoulders. "It's completely beautiful. I love it."

"And there's more. Come see my favorite."

We move past a pair of horses with hooves raised toward the sky then a statue of Apollo lying on a bed of leaves. Ten more steps and we're around a pair of lovers entwined in an erotic embrace and a fountain where a nymph poses with water streaming down her bare breasts.

We reach the private corner where Medusa waits, backed close to a wall covered with flowering vines, and I turn to watch Ivy's reaction. In the dim light, her eyes are shadowed, but the soft gasp as her fingers move to her lips assures me that she finds Medusa every bit as stunning as I do.

"You like?" I ask.

"She's perfect," she whispers, her voice thick with emotion.

"She is," I agree. "Like you."

"Edward..." My name is a warning. One I choose to ignore.

Instead, I lean in, pressing a kiss to her throat before whispering against her skin, "Leave the mask on, princess, but everything else comes off. I'm ready to see what's mine."

CHAPTER

Six

Ivy

What's *his*...

I could be *his* again. The invitation is clear in every glance and every touch, in the reverent way Edward's fingers skim across my skin and the affection in his voice as he says, "Now, Ivy. Take the dress and shoes off. I won't ask nicely again."

"Yes, sir." I hold his gaze as I reach for the straps of my dress and slide them slowly off my shoulders.

The heavy beaded fabric slides past my breasts easily, baring my skin to the cool air. The breeze whispers across my tight nipples, building the web of longing already knitting low in my body. I want Edward as desperately as I did outside the castle walls, but things are different now.

Now I've remembered how easy it is to talk to him, how clever and kind he is, and how he sees the world in a way no one else I've known ever has.

The Medusa statue is the perfect example.

Any other man would see a statue of a pretty woman with snakes coming out of her head and move on. But Edward saw the defiance in her expression and the knife in her hand. He saw the way the snakes writhe wildly around her haunted face, as if crying out in sympathy for this woman who was attacked by a god, betrayed by her goddess, and brought low through no fault of her own. The statue is a beautiful and heartbreaking call for justice, for innocence to be preserved, loyalty to be rewarded, and goodness to triumph over evil.

It's beautiful.

As beautiful as the mind of this man standing in front of me, his dark eyes devouring me, leaving no doubt that as far as he's concerned, I, too, am a work of art.

As I urge the dress over my hips, wiggling slightly to ease the tighter fabric at the waist over the swell of my bottom, the bars around my heart begin to melt. It isn't smart, it isn't safe, but damn it, he's Edward, and I can't seem to help falling for him all over again.

"You're stunning," he says softly. "The most beautiful thing I've ever seen."

I shiver as I step out of my gold sandals and stand barefoot on the small white gravel that carpets the courtyard. "Tell me how to please you, sir."

"Sit on the statue's pedestal." He reaches up, loosening his bow tie before shrugging out of his tuxedo coat.

I walk the three steps to the base of the statue and sit down, sucking in a breath as my warm ass meets cold marble.

"Chilly?" Edward tosses his tie to the ground.

"Yes, sir." My chest rises and falls faster as he strips off his shirt, revealing a thicker, harder version of the muscled chest I remember. "But I have a feeling you're going to warm me up."

"Not just warm you up, princess," he says, stepping closer. "I'm going to make you burn."

Before I can respond, he's knelt in front of me, curled his fingers around my neck, and pulled me in for a long, bruising kiss, crushing the fabric of our masks between our faces. I moan as I open for him, welcoming the assault of his lips, teeth, and tongue. He kisses me so hard I can feel our bones rubbing together beneath our lips, but I don't care if my mouth will be bruised tomorrow. This is the kind of kiss I need right now, the kind that assures me that there's no point in resisting.

No matter how many walls I build or how strong the bars around my heart, Edward will break them, bend them, destroy them. Because I am his. I always have been and I always will be.

"Spread your legs," he demands, his breath hot against my lips. I obey, parting my thighs to make room for him in between.

But clearly I don't part them far enough.

"Wider." Edward grips me behind my knees, spreading me so wide it sends a twinge of discomfort through my hips. "Don't fight me, princess. Let me in; give me control. I'm going to make it so good for you, I promise."

Biting my lip, I will myself to relax. Immediately the pain in my hips vanishes and the electricity building between my legs sizzles hotter.

"That's it." Edward strokes the insides of my thighs with his warm hands, making me tremble. "You're so sexy when you obey me, Ivy. Now put your hands on your tits. Touch yourself, baby. Make your nipples hard for me."

I obey, cupping my breasts in my hands and rolling my nipples lightly between my fingers and thumbs. But, though the touch is gentle, it still makes me wince in pleasure and pain. I'm so sensitive, so raw, and we've barely started. I swallow hard, backing off until I'm using almost no pressure at all, but I can't stop the whimper that rises in my throat. Waves of longing course from my nipples to the needy place between my legs, making me squirm as Edward spreads my knees even wider.

"You're already wet, aren't you, princess?"

I nod, tongue slipping out to dampen my dry lips as his thumbs dig deep into my inner thigh muscles, massaging the tight flesh beneath his fingers, slowly working his way from my knee up to where I'm already slick and ready.

"I can smell how hot you are," he murmurs, pressing a kiss to my neck before raking his teeth lightly across the skin, making me moan again. "So salty and sweet. I can't wait to get my mouth on you, to make you come on my tongue."

My hands fall to my sides, but he corrects me immediately.

"No, beautiful. Don't stop touching yourself. Pinch your nipples for me. That's it. Yes, like that, but harder."

I obey with a gasp, quickly becoming overwhelmed by sensation. I'm so keenly aware of him. Of the heat of his body and the smell of his skin—soap, sage, and Edward—and the restrained power in his touch as his fingers reach my sex and gently caress the swollen flesh of my outer lips.

"Have you ever had clamps here, sweetheart?" he asks, pinching my slick skin tight between his fingers.

I nod swiftly, quickly moving beyond language, beyond thought or reason.

"Answer me, Ivy. Tell me if you've ever had a man clamp your pussy before he fucked you."

"No, sir." My brow furrows in pleasure-pain as I continue to tease my nipples, and Edward continues to squeeze the lips of my pussy between his warm fingers. "I mean, yes. Yes, to the clamps. No, to the other. I've never gone that far with any of the men at my club. We've never had sex. I wa-wasn't ready."

"Are you ready now?" His thumb dips lightly into the well of heat between my legs before coming up to oh-so-gently circle my clit. "If I wanted to clamp your pussy before I fuck you tonight, would you like that?"

"Yes," I breathe. "I'm ready for anything you want to do to me, sir. Anything you want."

"Anything?" The pressure on my clit increases, making me gasp. I'm so close, dancing the razor's edge between anticipation and release, and he's barely touched me. "Are you sure about that, Ivy?"

"Yes." I meet his gaze, hoping he can see the desperation building inside of me. "Yes, sir. As long as you let me come before I lose my mind. I'm so close."

"I'm not going to let you come." His voice drops to a growl so deep I can feel it rumble through my chest. "I'm going to *make* you come. But first I want to show you another secret. Something that's going to make you feel so fucking good."

I blink, but before I can ask what he means, Edward grips me beneath the arms and lifts me into the air. A moment later, my back is against the statue's cold, hard thigh and something even colder and more insistent is nudging the skin near my tailbone.

I turn to look, but Edward captures my chin in his hands and turns me back to face him.

"It's the secret of this statue." He kisses me

softly, his tongue teasing along my bottom lip before he continues. "The snakes in the water at her feet aren't just beautiful to look at. They're made for things like this…"

His hands drop to my thighs, urging me to lift my hips and scoot back until the head of what feels like a cock made of smooth stone fits against the entrance to my sex. My eyes widen as I realize what he wants me to do, but I don't resist as he gently urges me to drop my hips, down…

Down…

Down…

…until I'm completely impaled on at least six inches of thick, solid marble.

"Oh God," I whisper, chest heaving as my pussy pulses and throbs around the cold stone. It feels so wrong, like I've been invaded by something foreign, penetrated by a creature that's not quite human, but at the same time it's so incredibly good. It's hot and dirty and strange in the best way. My inner walls grip and release, grip and release, undulating around the marble of their own accord, taking me higher, making me whimper again.

I'm on the verge of climax when Edward takes my hands in his and lifts them over my head.

"Hold on here." His voice is rough as he

wraps my fingers around what feels like part of Medusa's slim arm. "Don't worry, you won't do any damage. This statue was built to be used like this. Just like your beautiful pussy." His hand drops back between my legs, his fingertips skimming over my clit, making me gasp as he kisses me.

His tongue strokes against mine, fucking my mouth, claiming me as he rubs my clit harder, faster, until I'm rocking on the stone buried deep inside of me. It doesn't take long, however, to discover that I can't move more than an inch in any direction without the marble knocking against the bones of my pelvic floor. I'm pinned here, at the mercy of Edward's wicked hands. I should stay still and make sure I don't bruise something I'm going to want in one piece later tonight, but I can't stop myself from seeking the release I need so desperately. I buck into Edward's fingers and roll my hips, sending the blunt end of the stone that penetrates me into bruising contact with my G-spot.

I cry out, my head falling back as a violent wave of pleasure bolts through me.

"Not yet, Ivy." Edward flicks my clit lightly, making me groan.

"Oh please, sir," I beg against his lips as he kisses me again. "Oh please."

"Not yet, princess," he says, nipping at my bottom lip with his teeth. "I need to taste you first. I need to taste how badly you need to come."

I start to protest, to insist that I can't wait even though I want to. I want to please him as much as I want release, but I'm so close. I'm falling, tumbling, spiraling out of control. My lips part to confess my weakness, but before I can draw a breath, Edward pulls back and slaps my left breast—hard.

My eyes go wide, but he's already slapped my right breast, sending them both bobbing on my chest and a rush of white hot arousal throbbing between my legs. I go molten inside, burning hot enough to melt stone.

"Fuck, sir," I gasp, my nerves threatening to overload.

"You will wait." Edward slaps each breast again, harder this time, making me cry out as the fresh sting sharpens my desire to a knife point. "You will wait until I give you permission to come, Ivy. Do you understand me?"

"Yes, sir," I all but scream. "Oh God, yes, sir! Please, sir."

"You do please me." He cups my breasts in his hands, kneading the hot, tender flesh. "You please me so much, beautiful girl."

My head falls back, knocking against the stone as Edward takes first one nipple in his mouth and then the other, sucking and biting and teasing me, stoking the fire already roaring inside until I disintegrate in the flames. Until I'm nothing but one raw, exposed nerve desperate for release, and I lose sight of everything but the explosive need to come.

But I don't. I refuse to.

I fight to hold back as Edward's mouth moves between my legs, playing through my folds. I bite my lip and clench my jaw as he tongues my clit in beautiful, torturous circles and whispers that I taste like paradise. I cling to the stone above me, the statue's arm the only thing grounding me as I fight to wait, to last, to please this man who is about to give me the most intense, unbelievable, insane release of my life.

"You're so beautiful," he says, kissing my clit before he sucks it between his lips, making me cry out to the stars spinning overhead, praying for strength. I'm on the verge of losing the battle against my own pleasure, when Edward finally says, "Come, princess. Come for me."

With a groan that becomes a primal cry, my head falls back and my orgasm rips through me. My pussy locks down around the stone shoved deep inside, gripping fierce and tight, doing its best to prove that there is nothing more powerful than this pleasure. Not steel or stone or nuclear explosions or all the fiery suns burning in the sky.

I come so hard it feels like the skin is melting off my bones and I'm glowing white hot in the cool air, and then suddenly I'm outside my body. I watch myself writhe on the marble slipped between my legs as Edward kneels at my feet, worshipping my pussy with his wicked, wonderful mouth.

And for the first time since I started down this road, submission feels like more than an assertion of my post-Prescott-family identity, more than a way of saying that I call the shots as to who receives my obedience.

Tonight is explosive, but sweet. Savage, but sincere. Wild, but safe, sane, and exquisitely beautiful.

It might be twisted to find beauty in what most people would see as depravity—who lets herself be fucked by a statue and a man she hasn't seen in years?—but I do. I find beauty in this moment, this shared fantasy, and in the face of the serpent-haired woman who watches as my second release claims me with a ferocity that leaves no room for anything else.

There is no room for thought, no room for language, no room for anything but Edward and me and the magic.

CHAPTER
Seven

Edward

All I want to do is rewind time and relive every minute in this garden all over again, every moment of Ivy, fierce and magnificent in her pleasure, her submission. I want this first time tattooed into my memory forever. I want it so badly I'm tempted to stay between her legs until I make her lose control again, but there are voices coming from the tunnel leading into the sculpture court.

There's a chance that whoever is headed this way will miss the hidden side passage, but in case our time alone is coming to an end, I need to get Ivy covered.

In the past, I've never minded an audience. Sometimes I prefer one—there's something to be said for the phenomenon of group arousal—but I don't want anyone to see Ivy like this. She is shattered by pleasure, raw and vulnerable and incomprehensibly beautiful.

Anyone who laid eyes on her right now would fall in love at first sight, and I refuse to tolerate any competition for her desire or affection.

"We need to go, sweetheart." I pull away, shrugging back into my shirt and jacket.

"Go," she murmurs dreamily, clearly still drifting somewhere high above the clouds.

"Here, let me help you." I gently lift her off the statue, jaw clenching as I see the wetness she's left behind on the stone. I never imagined I could be jealous of a rock, but I am. I'm hard enough to give marble a run for its money and desperate to get my cock between Ivy's long, trembling legs.

So desperate that when her hip makes contact with my erection, I have to bite back a groan. It's becoming physically painful to be denied the sweet relief of her body, and I'm not sure how much longer I'll last before I have to take her back to our room.

"Arms up, beautiful." I set her back on her feet, holding her steady as I kneel and fetch her dress from the ground.

"What's wrong?" she asks. "Are you all

right?"

"I'm perfect." I smile as I slip the dress over her raised arms and the fabric glides into place. "I heard voices, and I don't want to share you, that's all."

She blinks, nodding as she runs a hand through her hair, smoothing her curls. "Me, either. I don't want to share you. This. Any of it. Is there another way out of this part of the garden?"

"Yes, but it's a bit of a climb." I hook the straps of her sandals with my fingers as deep voices echo through the darkness, confirming that intruders are headed our way. "Best let me carry your shoes."

"All right," she whispers, glancing over her shoulder. "Let's hurry."

"This way." I take her hand, holding tight as we jog across the gravel to the base of an ancient oak with roots clawing deep into the ground beneath us. When we reach the trunk, I form a basket with my hands. Without a beat of hesitation, Ivy places her foot into my makeshift step and reaches for the lowest branch, pulling herself onto it. I follow, swinging up beside her and pointing out the easiest route up through the limbs.

By the time two men stumble out of the tunnel, already half undressed and kissing as if they intend to devour each other from the neck down, Ivy and I have climbed high enough to step out on top of the wide wall surrounding the courtyard. There, shielded by the leaves, she pauses, turning back to watch as the dark-haired taller man falls to his knees, tearing at the top of his lover's pants.

I pull her close, her back to my front, and murmur into her hair, "Do you like to watch?"

"Sometimes," she whispers. "They're beautiful."

"They are," I agree. The blond man's cock is free now, fisted in his lover's large hand as the man in the gray mask brings his mouth to the swollen head and licks, teasing with his tongue in circles around the sensitive skin.

My cock throbs miserably at the sight. I've never been attracted to another man or been particularly turned on by the sight of two men fucking, but right now the knowledge that someone else's dick is being sucked and stroked while I pulse and suffer inside my pants, is enough to make my vision blur.

But as I've just shown Ivy, torture only adds to the fun.

I reach around her, slipping my hand beneath the neckline of her dress to cup her breast, feeling her heart thudding hard against her ribs. I make a gentle fist, pulling her tighter against me, hoping she can feel my pulse pounding every bit as fast. "But they lack imagination, don't you think?"

She glances at me over her shoulder, her lips curving. "You certainly don't."

"There's more where that came from, princess." I brush my thumb lazily back and forth across her nipple.

"Let me take care of you first." She reaches back, stroking my erection through my pants. "I want to make you feel good."

I glance past her to where the dark-haired man's mouth is getting well and truly fucked. His lover plows deep between the kneeling man's lips, shoving his cock down the other man's throat, grunting at the end of each thrust.

My grip tightens on Ivy's breast even as the brush of my thumb on her nipple grows whisper soft. "Do you think you're ready for that, princess? To have me in your mouth, down your throat?"

Her hand cups my ass, urging me closer as she arches her spine, nudging her tailbone against my erection with a rhythmic pulse that threatens to make my head explode. "I want you everywhere right now," she says. "Down my throat, between my legs, wherever you want to be, Edward, however you want to take me."

Biting the inside of my lip, I force myself to exercise restraint as I slowly guide the strap of her dress off her shoulder. I bring my hand to my lips, wetting my fingers and thumb before returning them to her nipple, making her gasp as I roll the tight bud between my newly slick fingers. "What about right here, right now? While we watch?"

She shudders. "Yes. As long as you promise not to fall off the wall when you come."

"Good point." I glance over my shoulder at the ten-foot drop to the ground on the other side of the wall. There are footholds that would make climbing down an easy task, but a fall from this height would be a good way to put an end to the fun.

I turn back, burying my face in her fragrant hair as I whisper, "I'll lie down to be safe. But don't worry, I'm fully capable of topping you, even if I'm on the bottom."

"I believe you," she says, breath rushing out. "I can't wait to have my mouth on you, sir."

"That makes two of us." With a last glance at the scene unfolding below, where the blond man pulls his lover's mouth tight to the root of him at the end of each thrust, I stretch out on the stones and open my fly, letting my burning cock bob free.

CHAPTER

Ivy

My first thought is that someone should carve him in marble, every inch of that beautiful length.

Edward's cock is even more stunning than I remember, nearly as long as my forearm and swollen so thick I'm not sure my fingers will be able to meet around it. A blue vein pulses along the ridge, echoing the hungry throb between my legs, and as he shoves his pants and boxer briefs lower, baring the entire length of him from root to rise, a drop of pre-come leaks from his tip.

His need is the most erotic thing I've ever seen, and I can't wait to be the one to bring him relief.

But first to torture him a little…

Biting my lip to hold back a moan of anticipation that might be overheard below, I kneel between Edward's spread legs, grateful that the top of the wall is a full three feet wide. There's plenty of room for me to brace my hands on either side of his hips as I lower my face.

I close my eyes, inhaling the clean, animal musk of his sex. It's an intoxicating scent, better than soap or cologne or anything manufactured in a lab. It's a smell that cuts straight through to the heart of me, triggering a powerful, primal response.

I breathe him in, and—*Yes. This. Right*— echoes through my head, but not in those words. The certainty and recognition coursing through me is older than spoken language. It's the vocabulary of blood and bone, of hour-long kisses that imprint the taste of the one you love on your soul.

Slitting my eyes, I soak in the sight of him before slowly extending my tongue and licking him from base to tip. His breath rushes out as I circle the head of his cock with lazy swirls, mimicking the way the slimmer man down below teased his partner.

I hear what sounds like a soft huff of laughter and then Edward's hand is fisting in the hair at the base of my neck.

"I'm going to take your mouth now, princess," he whispers, sending fresh heat rushing between my thighs as his cock nudges at my lips. "And then, if you're willing to bend your rules, I would very much like to fuck your pussy up here, hidden by the leaves. I promise no one but you and I will see a thing."

"Yes," I breathe, unable to imagine waiting until we're alone in our room to have him. My blood is still humming from our time in the sculpture garden, but while the marble was an illuminating novelty, there's nothing like the real thing.

Nothing like Edward and the way I feel him everywhere, his energy surging through my entire body and his spirit whispering through those secret, hidden places only he has ever touched.

"I'm ready." I sweep my tongue across his tip again. "Fuck my mouth, sir. Give me every inch of you."

"Slow," he cautions as he urges me down, his fist still tight in my hair. "Relax your throat and take a little more each time."

I part my lips, welcoming the invasion of his hot length as he presses between my lips. I want to moan in approval of the salty, sweet taste of him. I could probably get away with it—the men below are making their fair share of noise now—but I don't dare risk it. I would be mortified if strangers caught me watching them while I slide my mouth up and down Edward's cock.

I glance over, gaze landing on the blond man's buttocks as he flexes at the end of each thrust. He's fucking his partner's mouth so hard that logic tells me it must hurt, but the man on his knees doesn't look like he's in pain. He's groaning in pleasure, one hand braced on his lover's thigh and the other working between his legs, jerking his own hard length in time with his lover's thrusts.

The sight of his hand tugging his erection while Edward drives deeper into my mouth is indescribably hot. I've never enjoyed watching this much before, but then I've never been hidden away, spying without consent the way I am now.

It's so wrong, and I know I'll feel bad about it later, but right now I'm just turned on. So turned on my pulse is thundering in my ears and my heart is slamming against my ribs. As the blond man pulls out, losing control on his lover's chest, thick ropes of come shooting from his engorged length, my pussy clenches whip-tight.

And then the man on his knees pulls his partner down onto the gravel, spreading the come from his chest around the circle of his lover's ass, and I jerk my gaze away.

Damn.

I can't watch anymore. If I do, I won't be able to resist crawling over Edward and impaling myself on his cock. And it's not time for that. First I need to show him how dedicated I am to blowing his mind, to sucking him deeper than anyone has before.

I bring my hand to his swollen sac, playing with the heavy weight of his balls as he slows, giving me time to adjust as his thrusts reach the back of my throat.

"Shift forward and tuck your chin. Find the angle that feels right," he whispers, his voice tight. "Yes, just like that, sweetness. Swallow me; let your throat work me down a little at a time." His breath shudders out as I obey. "Fuck, yes, Ivy. *Fuck.*"

I'm tempted to smile as his vocabulary degenerates, but I can't because my mouth is full of him and my throat is full of him and a salty, acidic taste is clawing at the back of my tongue. But the discomfort only adds fuel to the fire.

I'm so hot, burning, and the deeper he pumps between my lips, the hotter I get.

By the time Edward brings both of his hands to fist in my hair, holding me locked in place as he bucks up into my mouth, fucking me every bit as hard and deep as the man in the garden took his partner's mouth, I'm flying. I'm also drooling and tears stream from the corners of my eyes, but I'm not embarrassed or ashamed.

I'm pleasing him, pleasuring him, unraveling this man who thrives on control. He's so wild—his breath coming in sharp, guttural rasps—that I'm certain he's going to come in my mouth.

But instead, Edward suddenly hauls me up his body by the hair and fuses his lips to mine. I don't have a spare second to wipe the saliva from my chin, but it's obvious that Edward doesn't care.

"You're so fucking incredible," he growls against my lips as he reaches between our bodies, sliding his fingers through my wetness. "I love the way you trust me. I want you to trust me—always—because I'm never going to hurt you again, Ivy, I promise."

He's talking feelings, breaking the conditions we agreed upon, but I don't care. All I care about is having Edward so deep inside of me that there's no room for anything but him.

"Show me," I whisper into his mouth. "Let me feel it."

Without another word, he reaches for the backs of my thighs, lifting me higher until his cock fits against where my body weeps for him. And then, inch by glorious inch, he fills me. Deeper, deeper until he's buried to the hilt, the base of his cock throbbing at my entrance. Each pulse builds the intensity of sensation, sending nirvana dancing across my skin, bubbling through my blood.

"Yes," I whisper, rolling my hips. "More."

He groans, placing a firm hand on my bottom, holding me still. "Wait. I want to remember the way you feel. Nothing has felt this good in so fucking long."

I shudder, ducking my head to hide my face in the curve of his neck. "You, too. It's so good. I could come right now if you told me to."

"Not yet," he says, fingers digging into my flesh. "Wait until I tell you to come on your cock." He cups my breast with his free hand, pinching my nipple hard enough to make me gasp. "Because it is yours, princess. I want you to know that."

I pull back, bracing my hands on the rough stone beneath his head. For a moment, I'm tempted to lift his mask and drop the game. I want to see him, just him, without the disguise.

But another voice in my head says that this is better.

The masks and the game give us something to hide behind. And maybe it's better to keep some things hidden here in this garden that seems to magically dissolve inhibitions. So I swallow the words rising in my throat, the ones that want to ask if he realizes how rare and precious it is to be able to come together so seamlessly after so much time apart.

Instead, I nod and whisper, "I'll come when you tell me to, sir."

He squeezes my ass tighter. "Lean forward. I need your tits in my mouth. Now."

I obey and Edward sets to work proving that he is, as always, the very best. He teases, licks, bites, and strokes, all the while keeping me pinned tight to him with the flat of his hand. And then he captures my nipple and sucks it deep, trapping the puckered tip against the top of his mouth.

My spine bows, and I have to bite my lip to keep from crying out as a wave of desire slams through me hard enough to make me flinch. My teeth dig deep into my lip, sending a flash of pain down my throat, but I don't ease up. I'm so close to losing control, to screaming, crying, begging for him to fuck me. My fingers are clawing into his shoulders through his shirt, and I'm wiggling desperately on top of him, but he's holding me too tight for the rolls of my hips to do any good.

"Wait." He swats my ass as he takes my other nipple in his mouth. The sound echoes through the otherwise quiet night, making my eyes go wide.

My gaze flies back to the sculpture garden, but the two men are gone. Evidently neither of them is a proponent of extended, prolonged, erotic torture. Unlike Edward…the wicked, wonderful son of a bitch.

"I hate you, sir," I hiss, moaning as his teeth drag across the sensitized tip of my breast.

"No you don't." He sounds amused, though I know he must be suffering as much as I am. His cock feels even thicker inside me, and his thighs are starting to shake beneath mine. "You love me. Admit it, Prescott."

I glare down at him, rethinking the wisdom of masks and broken rules.

How dare he do this? Now, when I'm clearly nowhere close to being in my right mind?

With a trembling hand, I flip his mask off,

deciding it's time for one of us to get real.

"You first," I demand, anger vibrating in my voice. But it's hard to hold onto my outrage. Now that the mask is gone, the moonlight is enough to reveal the tenderness in Edward's unguarded expression. My anger evaporates, leaving a haunting mixture of confusion and longing in its place.

"I love you," he says, without missing a beat. "Six years ago, I loved you enough to let you grow up without me hanging around to screw things up for you. I didn't want to be bad for you, Ivy. I had to give you time, but I hope I haven't given you too much. Because I need you in my life, princess. I need you so much."

I shake my head slightly, too stunned to speak. And then, finally, the pressure on my tailbone lifts and I'm free to move. I shift forward with a sigh of relief that's eclipsed by Edward's groan of pleasure as I slide back down, taking him deep.

"You're so good." His hands come to my hips, pulling me tighter to him as I rise and fall again. "You're the best thing that's ever happened to me, and I want to be the same for you. Let's happen to each other again."

My brow furrows and my lips part, but I can't form words. All I can do is hold

Edward's gaze as I ride him and all the old feelings come rising to the surface. They don't have far to travel. He's always been in my thoughts, my dreams, my fantasies, no matter how hard I've tried to move on and find someone else to give my heart to.

But there's never been anyone else. It was always Edward.

Edward when I was sixteen and he was the first person to tell me that I was beautiful. Edward when he was still a big-brother figure, warning me to be careful because boys wouldn't be able to resist a light that shone as bright as mine. Edward when I was twenty and finally able to convince him that I wasn't a little girl anymore. I was a woman who was ready to give him her body, her soul, her heart.

And it's still Edward now that I'm an adult who knows what she wants and who can admit to herself—for better or worse—that the answer is this man. He's what I want, him and only him. Because whether the time I have left on earth is long or short, it will never be as much time as I need to be with him like this.

I'm about to tell him, to confess that I still love him, too, but he hauls my lips to his and kisses me until I'm breathless. Soon I'm incapable of doing anything but holding on tight as Edward thrusts sharply between my legs, taking us both higher, higher, until he brings his lips to my ear and whispers,

"Now, beautiful. Come on your cock. Come on me, princess."

And I do. I come in thick, sticky waves, my inner walls squeezing him tight as his cock jerks inside me and the molten heat of his release fills me up. And it's so good I can't hold back the words rising in my throat, words and cries and a long, low, animal groan that certainly isn't the most delicate thing to ever come out of my mouth, but I don't care. I don't care about anything but how insanely good this is.

So good that when we're done I collapse onto Edward's chest with a sigh of complete and utter satisfaction. I'm so blissed out that I forget where I am until a loud voice at the base of the wall pierces the cool night air.

"Climbing on the historical landmarks is not permitted!"

Edward curses beneath his breath as I scramble off him so fast I misjudge the distance between his leg and the edge of the wall.

I realize my disastrous mistake, but I barely have time to yip in surprise before I tumble over the side and plummet through the air.

CHAPTER
Nine

Edward

Heart in my throat, I lunge for Ivy, but I'm not fast enough. My fingers snatch at the air inches from her arm, and then she's gone.

My chest goes so tight I can barely breathe as I tuck myself back into my pants and prepare to go after her. It's only ten feet to the ground, but that's far enough to break a bone, maybe even give her a concussion if she lands the wrong way.

And if she's hurt I will never forgive myself.

I should have exercised more control. I should have made sure we were on solid ground before sliding inside her. I should have remembered that this was Ivy, the woman who drives me fucking out of my mind, and taken the necessary precautions.

I'm still cursing my poor decision making when I look over to see two men in red masks detangling Ivy from a bush that must have broken her fall. She looks a little dazed, but blissfully unhurt.

"Are you all right?" I ask, just to be sure.

"Um…yes?" she says as she's set on her feet. The taller man reaches out, pulling a twig from her hair. "Yes. I'm fine." She bites her lip, casting a guilty look up at her rescuer. "I'm sorry. I… We…." She motions weakly toward me with a clearly forced smile. "We're both sorry. And thank you."

"Our pleasure, miss," the other man says before glancing my way. "Do you need assistance, sir?"

"No, thank you." I snap my mask back into place and then roll onto my stomach, dropping my legs over the side of the wall and finding the first foothold. A few seconds later, I'm jumping lightly to the ground and extending a hand to shake with one bouncer and then the other. "Thank you again for your help, and sorry for any trouble. We didn't realize the walls were off limits."

"No trouble at all, sir," the taller man says.

"Just try to keep your feet on the ground," his friend says in a crankier voice. "Or a little closer to it, anyway. I've never had a guest injured on my watch, and I'd rather not start tonight."

Ivy crosses her arms and tucks her chin, the picture of mortification. "We understand. And again, we're sorry."

"Very sorry," I agree with a smile, looping an arm around Ivy's waist, too thankful that she's in one piece to take issue with the guard's tone.

"Enjoy the rest of your night." The guard who pulled Ivy from the bushes nods my way, and the pair of them move along the path in search of other guests who might be bending the rules.

When I'm sure they're out of earshot, I lean closer to Ivy and ask, "Do you think the boys in the sculpture garden saw us up there spying and ratted us out?"

"Oh God, I hope not." Ivy's hands come to cover the eyeholes in her mask. "I'm already embarrassed enough."

I hug her closer. "Don't be embarrassed. There's no reason to be embarrassed."

"No reason?" She drops her hands to her sides with a huff. "We were doing it on top of a wall and then I fell *off* the wall, flashing two complete strangers on the way down. And to top it off, I have no idea where my panties are."

"It doesn't matter. Panties are overrated."

She steps out of my arms and turns back to me with narrowed eyes. "I'm serious, Edward. This level of shame wasn't on my agenda tonight."

I shrug. "I'm just glad you weren't hurt. Who cares what those men saw?"

"I care." She jabs a thumb at her chest, where one of her beautiful breasts is doing its best to escape again. "Just like I care that they saw us together. That's not something I wanted to share with other people tonight, and you know it."

I motion back toward the wall. "But you said—"

"Yes, I agreed in the heat of the moment," she says, pacing away, waving an agitated hand in the air. "I would have probably agreed to torturing baby bunnies in the heat of the moment, as long as you let me come afterward. That's why I asked you to agree to my conditions earlier, *before* we were both half naked. But instead of respecting my limits, you broke both of your promises in less than an hour, Edward. And that's not cool."

I nod, jaw clenching. "You're right. I'm

sorry."

Her shoulders rise and fall as she shakes her head. "You're sorry? That's it?"

"What else do you want me to say? That I wish I hadn't fucked you, or told you that I'm still in love with you? Because I can't do that, Ivy. Fucking you was the best thing that's happened to me in years, and I do love you. I never stopped loving you."

She presses her lips tight, her eyes shining in the dark ovals of her mask. "How can you love me? How can either of us know what's real on a night like this, in a place like this? This is…" Her hands flap helplessly at her sides, making her look like that sixteen-year-old girl I met the first time I accepted Aaron's invitation to come home with him, not long after both of my parents were killed. "This is Wonderland with sex, Edward. *Through the Looking Glass* with more voyeurism and toys."

"Wonderland for grown-ups," I agree, determined to get us back on the right track. "And what's wrong with that? You were having fun before we got caught by the wall police. Don't try to deny it."

Her eyes squeeze closed before she opens them again. "I'm not trying to deny it," she says in a softer voice. "And I do have feelings for you, but this isn't how I want to explore them. I'm not ready. Not tonight. For a moment, I thought maybe…" She trails off with a shake of her head. "But I'm not. I'm really not. And that's why I needed rules, a safe word, and some boundaries I could count on."

Fuck, she's right. I should have known better than to push her while we were playing. I *did* know better. I just wanted Ivy more than I wanted to be a good Dom. But I need to be both if I want to be worthy of her.

I take her hands, grateful when her fingers curl around mine. "I get it. And you're right, I should have taken your conditions as seriously as I would a safe word. That was a mistake. I messed up, and I'm sorry. I hope you'll give me a chance to make it up to you."

Her gaze falls to the grass at our feet. "You don't have to do that."

"No, I do. I want to. And I have an idea how to start." I tuck her hand into the crook of my arm. "Would you be willing to accept a glass of wine by way of apology?"

She glances up at me, mouth softening. "Make that a bottle for us to share, and you've got a deal."

"Done." I pat her hand as we start up the path toward the lights at the top of the hill. "And while we drink, I'll do my best to think of other ways to make amends for being a less than ideal Master of ceremonies our first time out."

She walks quietly beside me for a moment before she says, "You weren't less than ideal. While we were in the sculpture garden, I kept thinking…" She ducks her head. "I kept thinking that I'd never felt as safe during a scene as I felt with you. It was perfect. Better than perfect."

"And then I let you fall." I hate that it's my fault our night has taken a turn for the worse, but I know how important it is to own my mistakes.

"You didn't let me fall," she says with a sigh. "But I did fall. Falls still happen, despite all the best intentions."

And with those words, she tells me so much more than she knows. Making amends for my mistakes is one thing, but convincing a woman who's afraid to fall that love is worth the risk is another animal altogether.

But I'm not about to give up. Not tonight or tomorrow or any of the days after. Ivy is the one for me, the only woman who has ever made me feel like I'm exactly where I'm supposed to be.

Now I just have to prove to her that the magic we make when we're together is worth the risk, worth anything it takes to find our way back to each other.

CHAPTER
Ten

Ivy

The castle looks more like a church than I expected it to. The rough-hewn stones form frames for heavy wood doors and stained glass windows that give the structure a gothic feel. The vibe continues in the rose garden behind the building, where elegantly carved wooden chairs and tables for two are evenly scattered along a circular path.

At the center of the winding gravel walkway sits a large stone bar manned by women in red masks, and another beefy security guard type who stands watch by a buffet offering fruit, pastries, and other light snacks.

Edward orders a bottle of unfiltered

chardonnay from California's Alexander Valley that he assures me is even the more delicious for the funk we may find floating at the bottom, and we settle in at a table near a white rose bush. It's early in the year for roses, but tiny, tightly-curled buds already peek out from beneath the dark green leaves, promising that it's going to be a good year for beautiful things.

If I were the kind to believe in omens, I suppose it would be a good one.

But I'm not. I'm practical, logical to the bone. And every logical bone in my body is screaming that now is the time for caution, not romance or signs or second-chance daydreams.

"Would you like something to eat?" Edward nods toward the buffet.

I shake my head. "No, thank you." Suddenly feeling shy, I run a finger lightly down my wine glass, capturing a drop of condensation before it can pool on the table. Conversation shouldn't be harder than sex and submission, but it is. Letting a man dominate me is something that's become familiar in recent months. But letting down my walls, letting someone close enough to see the scars on my heart and the cracks in my confidence isn't something I've done in…

Well, in a long time.

Probably too long.

Maybe I should let Edward in, let him see that I'm not as perfectly pulled together and successful as he thinks I am, not even close.

We're basically alone. The high backs of the chairs and the darkness beyond the candle flickering on the table between us makes it feel like we're the only people in the world. If I strain my ears, I can hear voices murmuring from not far away, but I can't make out words. If I wanted to confess my secrets, this is as good a place as any.

But am I ready?

For Edward, all of this is normal, just another wild weekend for the playboy billionaire. But I'm out of my element and my depth. I've subbed at my club before, but that was a small, secretive deviance from the norm. I've never been a part of such a large public event. In some ways, this night is like a dream come true, but in others it's like the ocean before a storm—beautiful but dangerous, and just as likely to roll me under and crush me against the rocks as spit me out safely on shore.

"I'm opening a new hotel in Curacao later this spring," Edward says, breaking into my thoughts. "All private bungalows, built right over the water. You can see the fish swimming through windows in the floor. I would like to book a suite for you for opening week. I'll cover your flight, the room, and all your expenses. Consider it another small way of making amends."

I shake my head. "I've already taken too much, Edward. Even with my new raise, it will be years before I can pay you back."

He frowns hard enough to make his mask shift higher on his forehead. "We've already covered this. You won't be paying me back. My assistance came with no strings attached. Just like this offer. I have my own suite in the main operations building, where I'll be staying that week. You won't even have to see me if you don't want to. You can enjoy the beach and the pool and pretend you've never met the insufferable owner."

My breath rushes out. "You're not insufferable."

"Not a rousing endorsement, but I'll take what I can get." His lips curve. "Just promise me you'll think about it, okay? I want to bring good things into your life. Only good things. No stress, no mess, no sadness or regret."

No sadness or regret...

But how is that possible when there is already so much between us? So many things left unsaid, so many emotional land mines buried beneath the surface, primed and ready to explode?

Then dig them out, Ivy! At least try, for God's sake.

This is the only man you've ever loved. If now isn't the time to break the rules, take a risk, and jump into the waves, when is?

"I...I know I said I didn't want to talk about the past..." I break off, gazing down at the candle that flickers between us. The flame is small but strong, refusing to be put out by the cool breeze that gusts here on top of the hill.

Another sign. They're everywhere once you start looking for them.

Or maybe they're just everywhere when I'm with Edward.

I was never a fan of romance growing up. No matter how dark things were at home, I never fantasized about a handsome hero on a white horse riding in to save me. I didn't dream about that perfect guy; I dreamt about a life that was purely my own. About a tiny cottage by the sea, or an apartment high in a skyscraper in the city, where I could be anonymous and small in the best way. All I wanted was a place where no one would care that I was the daughter of a man who claimed

God had chosen him to tell the people of the world what worthless sinners they were. I was certain that all I needed to be happy was distance from the Prescott legacy and the chance to feed the spirit held within the walls of my own skin.

And then Edward walked into my life, awakening a longing that I hadn't known was there. He made me understand what Snow White and Sleeping Beauty must have felt when they opened their eyes for the first time after years under a witch's spell.

The first time Edward smiled at me, I'd thought, "So this is what they mean when they talk about butterflies." From day one, long before I'd realized that Edward and I shared the same sense of humor, the same values, or the same love for something more exotic in the bedroom, he had set my world spinning.

And he still does, making me feel like everything is moving too fast even though I'm sitting still.

"We don't have to talk." Edward covers my knee with his warm hand, reminding me his touch can be as comforting as it is erotic. "Or you can talk, and I can listen. I don't know if you remember, but I'm a good listener."

"Of course I remember." I meet his gaze,

and my heart starts pounding all over again, willing me to speak up.

It's time to stop being afraid, to reach out and give old dreams at least a chance to come true.

CHAPTER
Eleven

Ivy

"I remember everything about you, Edward." The confession emerges in a rush, releasing the floodgates on all the feelings I've held back for so long. "I was so crazy about you. I couldn't forget you, no matter how hard I tried. And believe me, I did try. I tried hard because after things ended I was really angry. And hurt. And sad."

"I was sad, too." The skin around his eyes tightens, but he doesn't look away. "But I don't regret ending it when I did. Yes, I could have handled things better, that's for damn sure, but it wasn't the right time for us. We were in two entirely different places and I—"

"And I was a dumb little virgin who

couldn't hang with the big boys." I toss back a too-large drink of my wine, humming around the mouthful of sweet, golden liquid before I swallow it down. "Yeah, I know. I get it."

"No. That wasn't it at all," he says, fingers digging lightly into my thigh. "Yes, I was more experienced, but that wasn't the reason it wouldn't have worked."

"Then explain it to me." I cross my arms. "Because from my end it felt like you were bored and cutting your losses. Ditching the stick-in-the-mud church girl before she could cramp your style any more than she had already."

"Not even close." His tone is brittle, angry, but I get the feeling he's more upset with himself than he is with me. "It wasn't about me, or what I wanted. It was about *you*. You were just taking the first steps out of your family's shadow. You needed to stand on your own two feet, to prove to yourself that you were strong enough to make it on your own."

I frown. "Really? That's honestly what you were thinking?

"Yes," he insists. "You were on the verge of casting off all your family's bullshit. The last thing you needed was another domineering man in your life, telling you what to do." He shakes his head. "And I wouldn't have been able to stop myself, princess. It's who I am. I can't help trying to bully the people around me into doing what I think they should do. It usually comes from a place of love—it certainly would have in your case—but I was afraid it would cripple you all the same."

"And who's to say I'm not crippled now?" I want to reach for my wine, but my throat is so tight I'm not sure I could swallow. "You were my one and only long term relationship. And we were only together six months. Sure, I've had my share of lovers since then, but I've never fallen in love. I haven't even gotten close."

"Me, either." He leans closer until I can feel his breath warm on my lips and my body begins to ache for him all over again.

"But that isn't because we're crippled," he continues softly. "It's because we weren't willing to settle for 'good enough' when we knew 'wonderful' was out there waiting for us." His thumb makes gentle circles just above my knee. "That's what I've been doing. I've been waiting for you. I thought the time was right to see if you might want to try again, but if I was wrong, that's okay. I can keep waiting. If there's even a long shot that you'll let me back into your life, I'll wait another six years. Or seven. Or ten. Whatever you need. Because I already know there's never going to be another woman I want to be with as much as I want to be with you."

My teeth dig into my bottom lip as my throat threatens to close completely. A part of me wants to throw my arms around Edward's neck and kiss him until he knows that the wait is over for both of us. But another part of me is thinking about the night I walked away from him, the night he let me go, and all the months after, when I wasn't sure I would survive the pain of losing him.

It was like he was dead, but…worse.

When my grandmother passed, I'd been devastated. She was the only person in my family who had ever made me feel unconditionally loved. She wasn't just a grandmother. She was a friend, a kindred spirit, a source of wonder, kindness, and truth in a childhood that had been lacking in all three. Losing her cut deep, but the wound healed fairly quickly.

Death, the only truly inescapable fate waiting to catch up with each of us, sooner or later, was the only reason she was gone. There was nothing else in the world that could have kept Gram from being there for me when I needed her. She loved me that much, so completely and selflessly that her love is still with me now, all these years after she breathed her last breath.

But Edward hadn't been dead. He'd been alive, out there somewhere being funny and kind and sexy as hell with another woman instead of me. Because I hadn't been enough for him.

It had taken a long time for me to believe that our split was his problem, not mine, and contrary to the cliché, time had never mended that wound. Time was just a cheap, bargain-brand Band-Aid, one that got sticky and gunky around the edges. Now, that Band-Aid is a part of me, a necessary piece of the puzzle, part of what keeps the Ivy Prescott Show up and running, concealing the fact that I never got over my first love and might never be able to love again.

Pulling it off would change my life. And there's no doubt it will hurt. A lot.

But not as badly as living without this man. The thought of walking away from Edward a second time is enough to make me physically ill, sending a sharp wave of misery surging through my chest and down to sour my stomach.

"One year." The words are out before I have any idea what I'm planning to say.

Edward's eyes widen. "You need a year to think?"

"No, I'll give this a year. *Us* a year," I say, making the rules up as I go along, faking it until I make it, the way I always have. It's a technique that's helped me achieve my professional dreams faster than I'd thought possible, and right now I can't think of any dream I want to become a reality more than this one. "And this time there's only one condition."

The relief and hope in his voice as he says, "Anything. You name it," makes my heart feel lighter than it has in a long time.

I reach up, pulling off my mask and placing it on the table, sighing as the breeze whispers across the newly bared skin. "No more hiding."

He tugs his mask off, dropping it to the gravel at our feet. "No hiding."

"And no more secrets," I say as he reaches for me, drawing me into his lap.

"No secrets."

"And no more doing what you think is best for me behind my back." I smooth his hair from his face, marveling that this stunning man is going to be mine again. "I don't think I'm as strong as you seem to think I am, but I'm strong enough to handle my own problems."

His eyes narrow. "I don't want you to handle your own problems. I want to help you handle them. And I want you to help me handle mine."

"Do you have a lot of problems?" I ask, lips curving. "The whole über-successful, beautiful billionaire thing isn't as easy as you make it look?"

"Absolutely not," he says. "I have more money than I know what to do with, Prescott, and a driving need to fix things and people and to generally stick my nose in where it isn't wanted or needed. I'm a meddlesome menace to society and in desperate need of someone to rein me in when I take things too far."

My smile widens. "I think that's called being a philanthropist. Or maybe just a nice person who wants good things for the people he cares about."

He grunts. "Which reminds me of *my* one condition—you stop talking about paying me back. I don't want you feeling indebted to me."

"All right." I wrap my arms around his neck. "But that's just where money is concerned, right? Because I've been thinking about tonight…"

He arches a brow. "Thinking what?"

"About orgasms," I say, dropping my volume as I add, "I've had at least two or three more than you've had, and that doesn't seem fair."

"Let me clue you in on a little secret, Prescott." He slides a hand beneath my ass as the other snakes around to cup the back of my head. "I fucking love making you come."

I smile against his mouth as he pulls me in for kiss. "Is that so?"

"It is." His lips move lower, kissing my throat. "Your orgasms are works of art, and you know I'm a collector."

"You do have an eye for art."

"I fucking love art. And I fucking love you, and I fucking love fucking you."

"I also feel strongly about these things." I sigh as he moves his hand from my neck to slip it inside the V of my dress, cupping my breast.

"And that's okay." He rolls my nipple in gentle circles, making me squirm. "You can continue to feel strongly, and I'll continue to love you until you're ready to love me back."

I bring my hand to his, stilling his fingers as I pull back to meet his gaze. "Thank you. I appreciate that. Truly."

"How much?" he asks, arching a brow.

"Very much."

"Enough to let me drag you up to our room and add a few more orgasms to my collection?"

I smile. "Absolutely. But are you sure you don't want to explore more, first? I know the Venus Ball only happens once a year."

"And it will happen again next year, and when it does, we will explore again," he says, standing with me still in his arms. "Right now I just want to be alone with you, princess."

"Me, too," I confess.

Games are all well and good, but there are times when it's better to be real. To be honest. To be naked in every way with the person who feels like home.

And hours later, after Edward has proven that he still makes love every bit as beautifully as he plays games, and we're lying tangled together in bed, I tell him that I love him and it's not scary anymore.

Turns out the cliché had it all wrong. It's not time that heals all wounds; it's orgasms. Lots and lots of orgasms, delivered by a man who loves you enough to consider your pleasure and happiness a work of art.

CHAPTER
Twelve

Edward

One Year Later...

They say time flies when you're having fun, and now I know it's true. The past year with Ivy has been a bullet train, flying by so fast there never seems to be enough time to take it all in.

So I've started taking pictures. Lots and lots of pictures, documenting every day of the life I'm lucky enough to share with the woman of my dreams.

It was actually Ivy's suggestion.

"You've got an eye for beautiful things," she'd said one afternoon as we were hanging a new Medusa painting I'd acquired on a business trip to Greece. "You should paint."

"And pigs should fly," I'd replied, dismissing the idea. "I can't draw a straight line with a ruler, princess. The one time I tried to paint it looked like a dog swallowed a box of crayons and then vomited them back onto the canvas."

"Ew," she'd said cheerfully. "Well, maybe photography, then? You can't make a picture look like dog vomit unless you intentionally find vomit to photograph. And I'd love to see what you see when you walk around the city. You always find the beautiful things no one else notices."

And so I bought two cameras, Ivy and I attended a weekend course on how to use them, and now our house is filled with even more beautiful things—photographs that document the days that pass so quickly when I'm with her.

But none of the photographs, even the ones Ivy let me take of her in our claw-foot bathtub, can compare to the woman herself, in the flesh.

Or in this hot as fuck dress…

Ivy picked out her own dress for the Venus Ball this year, a red strapless gown the same color as her hair, which makes her look like a column of flame. The orange and red feather mask she wears completes the ensemble, giving birth to thoughts of a phoenix rising from ashes. She is stunning, magical, and so fucking sexy I've been hard since the moment she stepped out of the bedroom.

And I'm certainly not the only one who's prepared to sell his soul to get his hands on her tonight. As we make our way to the castle gates, every man in attendance, and a few of the women, turn to watch. One burly man's head swivels so intensely I'm worried he's going to pull a muscle before he and his date get into the party. But I'm not jealous. There's no reason to be.

Ivy is mine, from the tip of her upturned nose to the ends of the perpetually cold toes she kept bundled in two pairs of my socks this winter because she insisted my socks felt warmer than hers.

Half of my socks are in her drawers, my T-shirts have been appropriated for walks around the neighborhood before work each morning, and the master bath has been taken over by dozens of bottles of curl-enhancing potions and creams Ivy insists are necessary to keep her hair from frizzing. She has left her mark on every room in my home, every aspect of my life, and I couldn't be happier.

Well, maybe I could be a *little* happier…

"Is your ass mine tonight, princess?" I ask softly as we find our place at the back of the line. "Is that my surprise?"

"No, it isn't," she says, smiling up at me. "Not that I would tell you if it was, because the whole point of a surprise is that you don't know what it's going to be. But it's definitely not your cock in my ass."

"What about my tongue in your ass?" I ask hopefully.

"That's repulsive, Mulligan. Really and truly."

I shrug. "I bet I could make you come that way, just from my tongue licking and teasing and fucking your ass. You should let me try."

"Keep it up and you won't get your surprise tonight," she says. "I'll make you wait until tomorrow when we get home."

I press my lips together, feigning greater irritation than I feel. "Fine. But then I'll be forced to retaliate by making you wait so long to come that you think you're going to die from it, princess."

She laughs. "You're going to do that anyway."

I grin. "I am. I love that you know me so well."

"Me, too." She presses up on tiptoe, stealing a quick kiss before we step forward, closer to the castle walls and all the fun we're going to have inside them.

There will be no drama, no worry, no falling off things or fretting about the future tonight. Tonight Ivy and I are completely in sync, in love, and happier than we've ever been. Our time at the ball will be one hundred percent pleasure, seven or eight hours of games and erotic torture, and, if I have anything to say about it, topped off with my cock buried deep in Ivy's beautiful ass.

I've had her in so many wonderful and wicked ways this past year, but she continues to deny me access to that part of her. Her ass is my final frontier, and I mean to conquer it—and show her just how incredible anal can feel when done properly—tonight.

My hand drifts down, cupping her bottom through the velvety fabric of her dress.

"It's not happening," she says, a sterner note in her voice. "I'm serious. I'm not ready, and we didn't bring lube."

"We could acquire lube," I say, knowing any erotic prop we desire is easily obtained at the castle's front desk. "But if you're not ready, then you're not ready. Just promise me this is still on the table for another night."

She shakes her head with a sigh, clearly thinking I'm crazy. "Yes, oh stubborn one.

It's still on the table for another night."

"Good. Because I need to fuck your ass before I die. It's on my bucket list. At the very top of it, in fact."

"I'll keep that in mind," she says with a laugh.

"Please do." I wrap my arm around her waist as I reach into my tuxedo jacket's inner pocket for our tickets. "Just in case we someday get into a terrible car accident together before my dick has made your ass's intimate acquaintance."

"I'll drag my shattered body out of the wreckage and make it happen," she promises dryly. "Scout's honor."

I laugh beneath my breath. "You're too good to me, princess."

"I am. But you're awfully good to me, too, sir," she says, the shift in her tone making it clear she's as eager as I am for the game to begin. "Where do you want to start tonight, Master Edward? In the gardens near the gates, or farther afield?"

I kiss the top of her head. "I want to start with a story, the way we did last time. Any hard limits for you tonight? Aside from the posterior-related ban already discussed?"

"No, sir." She leans into me, tilting her head back to whisper in my ear, "Though I would love to find somewhere private if possible."

"Me, too," I say, hoping she'll love the adventure I have planned. "I find I'm even less interested in sharing you this year."

She arches a brow. "Is this the same man who said he wanted to show everyone how pretty I am when I come on his mouth in that alcove back there?" She jabs a thumb over her shoulder, toward the shadows where I ambushed her one year ago tonight.

"Beautiful was the word I used. And that was before I remembered just *how* beautiful, and decided sharing that view with anyone else would be asking for trouble. I enjoy competition in most things, but not when it comes to you."

"As if anyone else would have a chance," she says, taking my hand as we reach the front of the line.

"Ditto, sweetness." I slip our tickets to the man in the red mask, and we step through the gates. On the other side, I squeeze her hand tight. "Think we can beat everyone else to the far side of the grounds?"

She reaches down to scoop her dress up in one hand with a grin, revealing a pair of red Nikes. "We absolutely can. I came prepared for climbing and running from security this year."

I curse softly in admiration. "I wasn't sure it was possible, but you just got twenty percent sexier."

"Race me over the bridge?" she asks, eyes glittering behind her mask.

"Ready in three, two—no fair! That's cheating, Prescott!" I call after her as she dashes down the path ahead of me. With a grin, I start after, following the sound of her laughter.

CHAPTER
Thirteen

Ivy

By the time I beat Edward over the bridge—it's hardly cheating to take a head start when my legs are at least four inches shorter than his—follow him through a maze of thickly planted trees near the brook, and hike to the top of a grassy knoll on the far side of the property, I'm starting to regret the ball gown.

"Next year I'm wearing spandex pants and a tank top." With a huff I drop the heavy fabric I've held bunched in my hands. The skirt swirls back around my legs, concealing my now mud-christened sneakers.

"Formal wear is required, my love," Edward says, motioning for me to follow him around a row of large rocks that block our view of whatever lies on the other side.

"I'll bedazzle the tank top, then." I laugh at the look Edward shoots me over his shoulder. "I love you. You're very cute when you're horrified by sparkles."

"I love you. And you're very cute when you're naked," he says with a grin. "When we get to the boat I want you to strip. I've always wanted to row a naked goddess across a moonlit pond."

I bite my lip, but before I can think of a reasonable excuse for disobeying a direct order during playtime, we clear the rocks, revealing a landscape that takes my breath away.

"Oh, it's magical." My gaze sweeps across the dark, moonlight-smudged pond where water lilies sleep in clusters near the shore. On a small island at the center of the pond, weeping willow trees trail silver leaves down to kiss the waves, and a single paper lantern hangs from a hook dug deep into the water, sending flashes of orange light dancing across the surface. "It's like a Monet painting at night. Or something from a fairy tale."

"Which is perfect. Because I have a fairy tale I want to tell you while we row." He takes my hand, leading the way down a stretch of sandy grass to a dock where three rowboats bob in the gentle swells. "I've never seen another soul on the island. We should have it all to ourselves."

"I can't wait to see it," I say sincerely, even as my mind clicks quickly through excuses to keep my clothes on and my surprise covered. "But would you mind if I waited until we're there to take off my dress? I know we were fast, but on the off chance someone else shows up while we're rowing across…"

"Of course." He leans in, pressing a kiss to my cheek before whispering against my skin, "but as soon as we're alone, the game begins. The next time I tell you to get naked, you'd better get out of that dress posthaste, or I'm going to have to punish you. So keep that in mind."

"Yes, sir." I smile as I climb into the boat and settle onto the wooden seat. I love a good spanking as much as the next girl, and am not above deliberately disobeying Edward to get one, but I'm not looking for punishment tonight. I just need to make sure he doesn't get a good look at my panties until we're alone.

"Tonight's tale comes from Denmark," Edward says as he grips the handles of the wooden oars and steers us away from the dock. "Have you heard the original version of The Little Mermaid?"

I lean back, bracing my hands on the sides of the boat. "Yes, I have, but I forget the finer details. I just remember that she turns into sea foam at the end because of that stupid prince she was in love with."

"He was a stupid prince," Edward agrees, because we always agree on important things like stories and art. "He didn't recognize that the mermaid was the one who had saved him from drowning. And because she'd traded her voice to the sea witch in exchange for legs, she couldn't tell him."

I shake my head. "If only she'd known how to read and write. Another reason education for women around the world, and under the sea, is so important."

"You make a good point, as usual." He smiles. "But the part of the story I've always found fascinating is how much the prince enjoyed watching the mermaid dance. She was evidently quite fetching on her new legs and danced beautifully, despite the fact that every step she took in her human body felt like knives slicing at the soles of her feet."

"I don't remember that part," I murmur, admiring the flex of his muscles beneath his coat as he works the oars through the water with deep, assured strokes. "You're very handsome when you're rowing, by the way."

"You're very beautiful when you're being rowed. Though I would have preferred you naked."

"Maybe on the way back," I say, heart beating faster as I consider how very different our return trip might be. It all depends on Edward's reaction to my surprise. "Was that the end of the story?"

"You know the way it ends," he says. "I'm more interested in the middle, and the way the mermaid gave her prince pleasure with her pain. Do you think she enjoyed it? That maybe it was good for both of them?"

"I hope so. Seems like the poor thing should have had at least some fun before she was turned to sea foam." I cock my head, ear dropping closer to my shoulder. "Do you intend to tell me a depressing story every time we come to the ball, Master Edward?"

He grins. "There's nothing depressing about this story. Because we're going to change the ending. Tonight, the mermaid's pain is going to feel so good she's going to beg her prince for another dose."

My nipples tighten beneath my dress. "Does this mean you brought the clamps?"

"Maybe," he says. "Guess you'll have to

wait and see. You're not the only one who traffics in surprises, you know."

But my surprise will be more exciting than nipple clamps.

At least, I hope it will. I adore clamps, but I *love* Edward—so much. I'm minutes away from knowing if I'll be listening to his strange, sexy stories forever, and the thought makes my stomach flutter. But thankfully the pond is small. There isn't time to get too nervous before we reach the island and Edward pulls the boat up onto the smooth white pebbles of the shore.

Neither of us speaks as he takes my hand and leads me through another gathering of willows, past fat camellia bushes heavy with blossoms, and into a clearing with more magic waiting at the center.

There, a statue of a mermaid reclines on top of a stone clamshell, chin propped on her fist as she gazes out across the water on the other side of the island. But this time it isn't the skill of the artist that takes my breath away; it's the carved wooden starfish that extends from the base of the mermaid's clamshell toward the ground.

The starfish is larger than I am, with five long arms, each one equipped with unbuckled leather restraints.

"Clothes and shoes off, princess," Edward whispers as he captures the zipper between my shoulder blades and draws it down. "Mask, too, this time. I want to see your face when you realize you're bound and completely at my mercy."

"Yes, sir." I wait for my dress to puddle at my feet then step free. I toe off my shoes and toss my mask to the ground, shaking my hair free as I pad barefoot across the leaves, wearing nothing but my red lace thong.

Once I reach the starfish, I glance over my shoulder to see Edward pulling off his mask, granting me a clear view of his face. I pause, soaking in the hunger and affection in his expression, certain I've never been so grateful for moonlight.

Now I just need the clouds to stay away for a few more minutes so the man I love can see the surprise I've sewn into my panties just for him.

CHAPTER
Fourteen

Edward

Ivy lies down on the bondage star and spreads her arms and legs. I bind her wrists then her ankles—pressing a kiss to the delicate bones as I pull the leather straps tight—and stand back, drinking in the view of my willing prisoner.

For a moment I forget how to breathe.

She is so beautiful, so perfect, and I have no doubt that I'm the luckiest bastard in the world. And not because her pale breasts, which seem to glow softly in the moonlight, are the most stunning pair of tits I've ever seen, or because the rest of her is equally flawless and sexy, and fucking her is an unparalleled pleasure that gets better every time I take her. It's because of her good heart and clever mind and the way she smiles just for me when she brushes my hair from my forehead in the mornings with a soft "beep, beep, beep." Her internal clock wakes her up at exactly six fifteen each day, and she insists on being my own personal, sweet, oh-so-sexy alarm clock.

I love her so much "love" doesn't seem like an accurate word anymore, but I've yet to find another to surpass it.

"Cat got your tongue, sir?"

"It does." I kneel on the ground between her spread legs, resting my palms lightly on her thighs. "I've run out of words. I think I'm going to have to start making up new ones."

"New words for what, sir?" She gazes down the landscape of her body at me, her eyes glittering as I lean in to press a kiss to her stomach.

I tongue the pulse beating there, circling her navel before making my confession against her sweet skin. "For how much I love you."

She sighs. "Me, too. Words aren't enough."

I cup her breasts in my hands, teasing her nipples between my fingers. "Then I'm only seeing one way this can go." I stand, lengthening myself on top of her as I brace my hands on the bondage star above her head. "I'm going to have to show you how much I love you with something better than words." I cover her lips with mine, kissing her hard and deep until she moans into my mouth.

I wait until she's squirming beneath me, arm muscles flexing against her bonds, before I kiss my way down her throat to her breasts, pressing her beautiful tits close so I can attend to both of her nipples at once.

"Yes, please," she cries out, arching closer. "I love your mouth, sir."

I hum low in my throat, showing her how much my mouth loves her nipples. I lick and suck and bite, making love to her breasts until she's panting beneath me. Only then do I reach for the clamps in my pocket, affixing first one, and then the other, to the taut, wet buds.

She cries out as I turn the screws, pinning her sensitive flesh tight between the metal. "God, sir. Oh please, touch me. I'm so wet for you."

"Patience, beautiful." My voice is rough and my cock is pulsing between my legs, but my hands are steady as I pull away, slowly stripping off my coat. "I have a surprise for you."

Her lashes flutter as her eyes open and her gaze meets mine. "Me, too. I almost forgot. Mine's hidden, but I have a feeling you're going to find it soon."

I dispose of my bow tie and shirt and reach for the close of my pants. "I'm sure I will. I don't intend to leave an inch of you unexplored. But first..." I step out of my shoes and drop my pants and boxers to the ground, baring my cock and the thick rubber ring stretched tight around the base of my shaft.

Ivy's eyes widen and her lips curve on one side. "A cock ring?"

"Not just any cock ring. It has a rubber pad at the top that's going to do wicked things to your clit."

Laughter bubbles from between her lips. And not just a little giggle—a throaty, full-fledged laugh that dances through the still air.

I frown. "This wasn't the reaction I was hoping for, sweetheart. But if you think you're going to get rid of my hard-on that easily, you're sadly mistaken. Nothing short of a nuclear explosion is going to keep me from fucking you while you're tied up and helpless to keep me from making you come again and again, until you regret laughing at my new toy."

She shakes her head, but she's still giggling when she says, "I'm not laughing at the toy. I'm laughing because…" She sobers, pressing her lips together "I'm laughing because great minds think alike. I brought you a ring, too." She shifts her hips back and forth, drawing my attention to the lacy red thong that's the only thing covering her nakedness.

Kneeling between her legs, I hold her gaze as I run my fingers beneath the waistband of her panties. "You did? And just where have you managed to hide a cock ring, Miss Prescott?"

"It's not a cock ring," she says, wiggling her hips again. "It's something even better. At least, I think it is."

I arch a brow as I draw her panties slowly from her body. "I'm not sure about that. I think we'll have to wait until you've felt what this ring is going to do to you before you make that call." I slide the fabric down her spread thighs until it is stretched to its limit. I'm ready to tear the thong in two when I see something catch the moonlight.

Something small and metallic…

I reach down, finding a silver ring tacked to Ivy's panties with two loops of red thread.

"I hope you'll put that one on, too," she says softly. "And maybe think about marrying me, Master Edward."

I shake my head as my chest fills with an aching, swelling, hopeful feeling. "Are you asking me to marry you, princess?"

"I thought about waiting for you to ask, but you know I struggle with patience, sir."

"You do," I say, throat tight. "But that's one of the things I love about you."

Fisting my hands in the delicate fabric of her panties, I rip them in two before tugging the ring from the lace and sliding it onto my finger.

"Is that a yes?" she asks as I stretch myself on top of her again.

"Yes." I kiss her hard as I fit the head of my cock to her entrance. "I can't wait to be your husband." I drive inside her, swallowing her soft cry, devouring her with my mouth as I ride her hard and deep. It turns out I have no patience, either. At least not at a moment like this.

"Oh, God, Edward," she cries out, straining against her bonds as her orgasm rips through her with enough force that I feel her inner walls locking tight around my cock. "You feel so good. So perfect."

"I love you, princess," I growl into the curve of her neck, too far gone to draw this out much longer. "So fucking much."

I manage to slow my thrusts long enough to release the clamps on Ivy's nipples, sending fresh blood rushing into the tight tips, making them even more sensitive. All it takes is a few gentle brushes of my thumb across her puckered flesh—once, twice, three times—as I grind against her to make her come again.

This time, as her pussy goes hotter, wetter, I let go, crying out in primal bliss as I come. My cock pulses so hard inside Ivy that by the time my orgasm is finished I feel like I've been turned inside out. There's nothing left but an empty shell, but that's all right. One look in her eyes is all it takes to fill me up again, to fill me with love and desire and gratitude for my sweet and wicked future wife.

"We'll get you an engagement ring on Monday." I kiss her cheek. "I want you tagged as off the market as soon as possible."

She smiles. "Good. I like being tagged by you. And that cock ring? Best thing *ever*."

I gaze down at her blissed-out expression, unable to help feeling a little smug. "I know what I'm doing, Prescott."

"You do," she says with a happy sigh. "I'm a lucky girl."

"Does this mean I have permission to slip in the butt plug I brought? I promise you, it's going to rock your world the next time I make you come."

She rolls her eyes, but she's still smiling when she says, "Yes, love. What better way to celebrate our engagement than with a butt plug?"

I grin. "I think I just fell a little more in love with you, Mrs. Mulligan."

"I like the sound of that." She hums happily into my mouth as I kiss her lips.

And then I kiss her neck and her shoulders and the soft skin beneath her breasts. I kiss her belly and her thighs and between her legs, where she is so slick from the evidence of our combined enthusiasm for fucking each other that the plug slides in easily. And when I make her come on my tongue with the plug in her ass, I can tell she's a fan. By the time I slide my cock inside her, she's wild, out of her mind with pleasure, swearing nothing has ever felt so good as coming hard with my cock and the plug both buried deep inside.

Afterward, I'm not shy about telling her "I told you so," and she's not shy about telling me that she's ready for my cock to claim that final frontier.

And then it's my turn to be driven out of my mind.

We don't leave the island the entire night. We make love again on the pebble beach and lie side by side in hammocks next to the water, planning an October wedding because we both agree autumn is the sexiest season. I have Ivy again in my hammock, slowly and carefully with her on top, and this time no one falls.

She simply lays her head on my chest afterward, and we watch the sun rise over the water, savoring the first day of our forever.

Love sexy, flirty, dirty love stories?
Sign up for Lili's newsletter and never miss a new release or sale:
http://bit.ly/1zXpwL6

Keep reading for a sneak peek of Dark Domination and meet Jackson Hawke, a magnificent, sexy as hell Dominant who will own your e-reader. (Dark Domination is free!)

Sneak Peek
Dark Domination by Lili Valente
Now free on all platforms
Excerpt c. 2016

Hannah's eyes flew open and her lips parted in a scream, but the enormous man straddling her pressed his hand tighter to her lips, muffling the sound.

She jerked her arms downward, ready to fight him off, only to discover that her wrists were tied to the headboard. Terror rushed through her and her pulse sped, setting her heart to slamming against her ribs as she tugged harder on her bonds. But the rope biting into her wrists assured her she wouldn't be able to fight her way free.

She was bound tight, powerless to protect herself from whatever this man intended to do to her.

"Relax, princess. It's just me." The man leaned down, the water dripping from the end of his nose, landing on Hannah's cheek, making her flinch. "I came in through the window. I thought I'd make that fantasy you were telling me about a reality."

Hannah swallowed, her thundering heartbeat slowing a bit as she understood what was happening.

She wasn't being attacked by an intruder. This man must be Harley's guy of the moment, and he *clearly* thought he was straddling her sister. Once she cleared up the misunderstanding, he'd untie her and she could show him to the door. They'd both be embarrassed, no doubt, but she wasn't about to be raped or murdered.

The realization made her whip-tight muscles sag with relief, an action she realized too late that the man took as an invitation to continue living out Harley's bondage fantasy.

"I've been dying to touch you all day," he said, his dry palm moving from her mouth to her breast, teasing her nipple through her thin tee shirt, drawing a gasp from her throat.

She expected his touch to feel foreign and unwelcome, but his fingers were gentle, teasing her with a sweetness that made her arch into his warm hand. Electricity shot from her breast to coil between her legs, the sensation intensified by the feel of the rope digging into her wrists as her biceps tightened reflexively in response to the stranger's confident touch.

"God, the sounds you make drive me crazy," the man said, pinching her nipple tight enough to make her gasp again.

"No, please, I'm not—" Hannah's words ended in a moan as he pushed her shirt up and bent lower, tugging her nipple into the warm, wet heat of his mouth. His tongue flicked and teased, flooding her body with pleasure and longing so intense she was panting by the time he transferred his mouth to her other breast, sucking and nibbling at the aroused skin as his big hand slipped down the front of her panties, finding where she was already wet.

Wet, from her *sister's boyfriend's* mouth on her breasts. And now his fingers were sliding into where she ached, making her shudder.

If she didn't stop this soon, it would be too late. There would be no avoiding tragedy, there would be only shame and the nightmare of confessing to her sister and this innocent man that she'd done something unforgivable.

"Stop, I'm not Harley." She tensed her thighs only to relax them a second later when she realized her locked muscles were trapping his fingers inside her embarrassingly slick sex.

"No, you're not," he said, driving his fingers in and out of her as he trapped her nipple between his teeth and bit down, making her cry out in pain before he soothed away the hurt with his tongue.

"You're my little slut," he continued in his deep, sexy rumble of a voice, his fingers still busy between her legs, making the tension coiling low in her body fist even tighter. "And I'm going to fuck you until you scream."

"No, please," Hannah said, excitement and fear dumping into her bloodstream simultaneously, making her feel like she was being deliciously, torturously torn in two. "I'm not Harley, I'm—"

This time, he silenced her with a kiss, his tongue pushing between her lips, demanding entrance to her mouth. He tasted of something smoky, hard cider, and the ocean on a day when it isn't safe to go into the water. His kiss was dangerous, wild, and unlike anything Hannah had experienced before. He didn't tease or test her; he fucked her mouth with his tongue, the thick muscle mimicking the movements of his fingers between her legs, bringing her to the edge faster than she'd imagined possible.

She'd had trouble tumbling over in the past. But her former boyfriends had always been sweet men and often too-tender lovers.

This man might be sweet—she had no way of knowing what he was like outside the bedroom—but he wasn't tender. He was demanding, controlling, the type of man who didn't hesitate, didn't change course, didn't stop until the job was done. There would be no easy escape from this bed, she knew it even before he hooked his fingers inside of her, coaxing her into an orgasm that had her bowing off the bed, screaming into the hot, hungry mouth still devouring her own.

Her body clenched down, liquid heat gushing out to dampen her thighs as pleasure rocketed through her core and his tongue continued to fuck her mouth, building her need again even as her pussy still throbbed and clutched at his thick fingers.

By the time he grabbed her behind the knees, forcing her legs up and out—until her knees were in her armpits and she was bared to him, from her ass to her dripping sex—she was beyond words, beyond identity, beyond awareness of anything but the blunt head of his engorged cock hot at her entrance.

Fear flashed through her for a moment— she was on the pill, but she'd never had sex without a condom before—but then he was gliding into her, shoving through her swollen flesh, stretching her so wide she wasn't sure she'd ever be the same again.

She moaned, pain and pleasure warring within her as he claimed her in one long, slow stroke. He was enormous and so thick her body fought to eject him, to banish the burning sensation he caused between her legs. But he kept coming. And coming and coming, until she swore she could feel him in her belly, in her lungs. He was everywhere, his hot thickness filling her up until there was no room for anything but him.

She tried to breathe deeper, to center

herself, to hold on to that sacred, hidden kernel of her soul no man had ever touched, but she couldn't find it.

There was only him, his heat, his rain and campfire smell, and his need, spearing her in two, insisting she take everything he had to give.

"Look at me," he said, holding still inside her, his voice demanding she obey. "Look at me."

She lifted her eyes to his, a ragged sob escaping from her strained throat. At this angle, the light from the bathroom hit his face and she was granted her first good look at him, this stranger who was buried inside her, and it all but stopped her heart. He was beautiful—strong, rugged features softened by full lips and dark eyes that burned with passion and intelligence. He was as stunning as all of Harley's men, but there was more to him than a handsome face or a gorgeous body. There was something in his eyes, something that made her want to know him, to please him.

"I know what you want," he said. "But I

can't go there until you tell me that you're mine." He paused, looking so deep into her she couldn't believe he didn't see that she was an imposter.

But in the long, breathless moment that their eyes held and all of Hannah's secrets and fears seeped into the air between them, his gaze only gentled.

"Because you are mine," he said softly, his voice as tender as his cock was merciless. "Your pleasure belongs to me, your pain belongs to me. I want it all, Harley. All of you. Don't fight me anymore. Give it to me. Give it all to me."

Hannah's breath rushed out through her parted lips, but she didn't know what to say, how to tell him she was a liar when this moment felt so real, so right.

"You can trust me." He flexed his buttocks, forcing his cock impossibly deeper, making her groan in pleasure. In pain.

Pleasure-pain. They were one and the same with this man and she wanted nothing more than to give him what he wanted, whatever he wanted so long as he would never stop hurting her, healing her, possessing her in a way she'd never realized she wanted to be possessed until this stranger had claimed her for his own.

But she wasn't his and he wasn't hers.

He belonged to her sister and this was so wrong that "wrong" wasn't a big enough word to describe it—this betrayal, this sacrilege, this terrible, terrible thing she'd allowed to happen. She should have fought harder, screamed the truth until he understood she wasn't playing games.

Now it was too late, and she hated herself for it.

"Please," she said, tears filling her eyes. "Forgive me."

"For what, princess?" His warm palm cupped her cheek with a sweetness that threatened to break her heart all over again.

"I can't..." She swallowed, searching for the strength to tell him the truth, but she couldn't, not when she was exposed, so vulnerable, and so intimately connected to this man that she couldn't tell where he ended and she began. "I can't tell you. Not now."

"Now is the time to tell me anything," he said, leaning down, his lips hovering above hers as he shifted his hips, pulling out until she was acutely aware of all the places that ached in his absence before pushing back into her again, summoning another hungry sound from her throat. "Everything. I'm ready for your secrets."

"No, you're not," she whispered, shuddering as he began to roll his hips, nudging her clit with his pubic bone again and again, building the need swelling inside of her.

"I'm not a fool." He captured her nipple between his fingers, tugging it in time to the undulating rhythm of his hips. "I know you've been hiding things from me. It doesn't matter. What matters is right now. Tell me you're mine and we'll figure the rest out together."

"Stop, please," she said, teeth digging into her bottom lip as she strained against her bonds, but the rough rope against her skin only made her hotter, wetter. "I can't think. I can't—"

"Don't think," he said, his grip tightening on her nipple as he rode her harder, until she was quivering beneath him, so close to the edge she knew she could go at any moment. "Feel. Feel how real this is and tell me you're mine. Tell me and I'll do all those things you've been dreaming about."

He shifted his head, whispering into her ear, his breath hot on her skin as he fucked her with long, languid strokes that completely unraveled her mind. "I'll spank you and mark you and fuck you so hard you won't be able to sit down for days without thinking about how I used you." He pressed a kiss to her throat, where her pulse raced. "Isn't that what you want?"

Hannah nodded breathlessly. She had never even imagined things like that, but suddenly, lying beneath this man, she wanted all the wicked things he'd promised and more. She wanted to be turned over his knee and punished for the lies she'd told. She wanted him to hurt her for letting him believe she was someone she wasn't, and then she wanted him to take the pain away with his beautiful mouth.

That exquisite mouth that made her

shudder now as his teeth dragged lightly over the skin at her throat.

"Then say it," he said. "Give yourself to me. Tell me you're mine."

"I'm yours," Hannah said, the words out of her mouth before she could stop them. "I'm yours. Forever. Yours."

"Fuck yes, princess," he moaned, thrusting faster, deeper, demanding her pleasure. "Come for me. Come on my cock. Let me feel you."

Hannah's head fell back as she came with a sound that wasn't cute or ladylike. It was wild and base, a cry of animal satisfaction that ripped from her throat as her pussy clutched at her stranger's pistoning cock, demanding his orgasm with the same assurance that he'd ordered her own.

He came crying out her sister's name, his thickness jerking hard inside of her, the feel of his scalding heat soaking her insides sending her soaring a third time. Lights danced behind her tightly closed eyes, and somewhere deep inside of her, things she needed to live lost purchase and floated away from their moorings. She was adrift, helpless to defend herself, totally at the mercy of this man who gently untied her arms and kissed the red welts on her wrists.

And she didn't even know his name.

Hours later, after he'd had her again—this time with his hand fisted in her hair while he took her from behind, his rough use making her feel safer than every considerate kiss from every ex-boyfriend she'd ever had—that's all she could think about. She didn't know the name of the man who kissed her like she was his world before climbing back out the window he'd crept through hours before.

And she wasn't going to find out until tomorrow, when she would be forced to come clean to her sister and confess the nightmarish thing she'd done.

Harley might actually forgive her—she didn't tend to get too attached to her lovers, especially the summer boys she used to entertain her between epic trips abroad—but the stranger would hate her. He was in love with her sister. He thought he'd been making love to Harley, not a complete stranger.

As Hannah lay in the dark, in sheets that still smelled of sex and sweat, she was forced to admit that she was a terrible person. She wasn't the good twin, after all. She was weak and selfish and obviously unfit to become a psychiatrist and counsel troubled kids, not when she was so messed up in the head that she'd slept with her sister's boyfriend.

The first time, he hadn't given her time to protest, but she could have stopped things before they came together again, before he held her on his chest and promised she would always be under his protection, or before she whispered "I love you, too" as he eased out onto the tree limb beneath the second story window.

Liar. She was such a miserable liar.

She didn't know if Harley loved the man, but Hannah barely knew him. It was impossible to love a man you had just met and barely spoken to aside from some scalding hot pillow talk.

She knew that, but as she got up to put the sheets on to wash and start a pot of coffee—sleep was going to be impossible, might as well help the insomnia along—she couldn't help wishing that she didn't have to tell her stranger the truth. A selfish, wicked part of her secretly hoped that Harley would never come back to her summer apartment, that she would hop the next flight to Paris and disappear the way she sometimes did, usually right when Hannah needed her the most.

And then Hannah could meet the man again, learn his name, and start figuring out what it would take to make him hers.

In the years to come, she would think of that selfish, wicked wish again and again, wondering if wishes like that had a power others didn't. Wondering if her greedy longing was the reason her sister had been murdered and Hannah would never see her best friend's face again.

Even when her Aunt Sybil spirited her away from Harley's very private, very secret wake, insisting it was past time she learned about the darkness that haunted their family, Hannah couldn't bring herself to blame fate or her father's enemies for her sister's death.

She would never forget that one wonderful,

terrible night, or that she had wished that Harley would disappear and that hours later she had.

Forever.

Dark Domination is #free on all platforms!

Learn more at Lili's website:
http://www.lilivalente.com/#!dark-domination-is-free/c1yju

Acknowledgements

First and foremost, thank you to my readers. Every email and post on my Facebook page have meant so much. I can't express how deeply grateful I am for the chance to entertain you.

More big thanks to my Street Team, who I am convinced are the sweetest, funniest, kindest group of people around. You inspire me and keep me going and I'm not sure I'd be one-third as productive without you. Big tackle hugs to all.

More thanks to the Facebook groups who have welcomed me in, to the bloggers who have taken a chance on a newbie, and to everyone who has taken time out of their day to write and post a review.

And of course, many thanks to my husband, who not only loves me well but also supports me in everything I do. I don't know how I got so lucky, man, but I am hanging on tight to you.

Tell Lili your favorite part!

I love reading your thoughts about the books and your review matters. Reviews help readers find new-to-them authors to enjoy. So if you could take a moment to leave a review letting me know your favorite part of the story—nothing fancy required, even a sentence or two would be wonderful—I would be deeply grateful.

About the Author

Lili Valente has slept under the stars in Greece, eaten dinner at midnight with French men who couldn't be trusted to keep their mouths on their food, and walked alone through Munich's red light district after dark and lived to tell the tale.

These days you can find her writing in a tent beside the sea, drinking coconut water and thinking delightfully dirty thoughts.

Lili loves to hear from her readers. You can reach her via email at
lili.valente.romance@gmail.com
or like her page on Facebook
https://www.facebook.com/AuthorLiliValent
e?ref=hl

You can also visit her website:
http://www.lilivalente.com/

Also By Lili Valente

Sexy Flirty Dirty Standalone Romantic Comedy:

Magnificent Bastard
Spectacular Rascal
Incredible You

The complete To the Bone Series is Available Now:

A Love so Dangerous
A Love so Deadly
A Love so Deep

The complete Under His Command Series is Available Now:

Controlling Her Pleasure
Commanding Her Trust
Claiming Her Heart

**The complete Bought by the Billionaire
Series
is Available Now:**

Dark Domination
Deep Domination
Desperate Domination
Divine Domination

**The complete Dirty Twisted Love Series
is Available Now:**

Dirty Twisted Love
Filthy Wicked Love
Crazy Beautiful Love
One More Shameless Night

**The complete Bedding the Bad Boy
Series is Available Now:**

The Bad Boy's Temptation
The Bad Boy's Seduction
The Bad Boy's Redemption

The Master Me Series (Standalone Novellas):

Snowed in with the Boss
Masquerade with the Master

Made in the USA
San Bernardino, CA
26 December 2017